In Grandfather's Barn

In Grandfather's Barn

BY

WILLIAM SEARS

BAHÁ'Í PUBLISHING TRUST
WILMETTE, ILLINOIS 60091

Bahá'í Publishing Trust, Wilmette, Illinois 60091-2844
Copyright © 1997 National Spiritual Assembly
  of the Bahá'ís of the United States
All rights reserved. Published 1997
Printed in the United States of America

00 99 98 97   4 3 2 1

Design by Patrick J. Falso

Library of Congress Cataloging-in-Publication Data
Sears, William.
        In grandfather's barn / by William Sears.
                p.   cm.
          ISBN 0-87743-257-0
          I. Title.
PS3569.E195I5   1997
813'.54—dc21

                                96-52145
                                      CIP

Contents

1

A City of Whited Sepulchers

The whole town of Green Valley smelled like a flower garden when I came out of church. And there was even a whiff of Sunday chicken being roasted in the parsonage next door.

Not all good things are inside the Church, I told myself with a chuckle. Then I quickly made the sign of the cross. I knew better than to fool around with the powers of heaven. I'd learned that in Sunday school from Father Hogan, who was really a very nice man when he wasn't reminding you that God is a policeman.

We used to have some pretty cheerful Sunday school classes with Miss Poppenburg. She was my grade-school teacher at Ben Franklin, and she also taught our Sunday school class at St. James. Eivar Olson, who was on the school board, said it was a clear case of the church sticking its nose in the affairs of the state, and he was against it. But that was because he never had Miss Poppenburg in class.

Miss Poppenburg was pretty and a lot of fun. She could make Pharaoh chasing Moses through the Red Sea sound like Billy the Kid with a posse after him. Sunday school was great until Father Hogan showed up and started shaking his finger at us.

Father Hogan was fiercer than any of the statues in church. One wave of his big, pudgy finger put an end to our games of spiritual cops and robbers. It even turned out the lights in Miss Poppenburg's eyes.

Funny, Father Hogan was as good-natured as the inside of a hickory nut when you met him out on the street, but inside the walls of the church, it was as if that nut had been dipped into some dark, bitter chocolate.

I won't say there was rejoicing in the streets when Father Hogan was transferred to Duluth, but I *will* say that we all shook hands quietly with each other in Sunday school the day we heard the news. Miss Poppenburg made believe that she was studying the first chapter of Isaiah and couldn't see us. She didn't look really happy or anything, but she didn't look like she was going into mourning either.

Father O'Malley was our new priest. He was much younger and came from Notre Dame. Father O'Malley made religion understandable to us because he taught us how to tackle and block and carry the ball and everything.

I think Father O'Malley was on better terms with God than Father Hogan was because he laughed a lot. My own father said there was a lot more to religion than an off-tackle smash and a belly laugh, but I didn't agree with him at all.

My father changed his mind the Sunday Father O'Malley gave his first sermon. The sermon took our whole town by storm. It brought on at least ten different crises.

As we came down the church steps that Sunday morning, I could tell that my father was pleased.

"Great sermon!" he told Mother. "Wonderful, simply wonderful!"

Mother nodded.

Whenever Father talked to my mother, she nodded—even when she wasn't listening. I could always tell when Mother turned herself off, but my father couldn't, even after all the years they'd been living together. I guess he just couldn't believe that everybody wasn't crazy about hearing his every word. My mother could nod, grunt, say "Hmmm?" and "Yes, Frank," and go right on with her own business, and my father would be none the wiser. He thought Mother was very understanding and keenly interested in his every word.

I caught on to that before I was ten. My father was nearly forty and still didn't know Mother was in another world while he was telling her all those important things about himself. Of course, I wasn't as wrapped up in my father as he was. I was mostly wrapped up in my own more serious and important problems.

I've noticed that people are mostly interested in themselves, even when they show you how *fascinating* they think you are. It's mostly to get you to notice the real truth about how great they themselves are.

When you run across somebody like my grandfather, who turns out to be really interested in you, it throws you right out of whack. But it sure feels good!

Mother was "Hmmming" and "Yes, Franking" all the way down the church steps that Sunday. Father expanded under what he thought was her devoted attention.

"By the lord Harry!" Father laughed. "That sermon hit the nail right on the head. Imagine Father O'Malley being in town only one week and being able to pick out Sam Raffodil like that. Amazing!"

Mother looked surprised. Father had finally gotten her attention. "What makes you think Father O'Malley was talking about Sam Raffodil?"

"Didn't you get it? Father O'Malley was talking about whited sepulchers," Father explained, "outwardly fair, but inwardly foul. If that's not Sam Raffodil, Sr., to a *T*, I'm a six-winged seraphim!"

Now I was surprised. I thought Father O'Malley was talking about Sam Raffodil, Jr. I was really impressed with Father O'Malley's seeing through Sam, Jr., in so few days. Now *there* was a *real* viper, or I was not a six-winged whatever my father said.

I was pretty shocked to find out that almost everybody in our church thought Father O'Malley was talking about a different person. Even the mayor of Green Valley, Mr. Elmo Kearns, was fooled, and Mayor Kearns was supposed to be smart. His Honor paraded out of church with a big Sunday vote-getting smile on his face. The mayor gave his wife an affectionate embrace when he saw everybody watching him. His hug almost frightened his wife back into church. Mayor Kearns was famous in our town for being more loving to his constituents than to his own family. Grandfather said his family didn't even vote for him. This was only a town joke, of course. The Kearns family would be too afraid not to.

Mayor Kearns laughed out loud and told his wife in a booming voice meant for everybody, "I like this young Father O'Malley. He has a great sense of citizenship. And if he keeps after Jebez Casey for a few more Sundays, he may do this town a world of good. Yes, sir, a world of good!"

Jebez Casey was the one who always ran against Mr. Kearns for mayor. Mrs. Kearns gave her husband a meaningful look and said, "Maybe Father O'Malley had someone quite different in mind."

"Nonsense!" the mayor boomed. Mayor Kearns was wearing the same menacing look he used at meetings when he asked, "Are there any questions?" and no one dared ask any. Mayor Kearns put a fat finger under his wife's chin and lifted her face toward his to explain how she should feel. "Whited sepulcher. Outwardly fair, but inwardly foul. That's Jebez Casey. Who else *could* he mean?"

Mrs. Kearns stared at her husband for a long time. I'm not sure what her look said. I only know it was sort of pathetic. The mayor's look told his wife that she had just heard the party line and that she'd better believe it. I won't say Mayor Kearns gave his wife a mean look, exactly, but I know if he'd been my father, I wouldn't have used that moment to ask for an increase in my allowance.

The moment the crowd had begun to file out of church, the mayor's whole face had lit up in a flash of great, good cheer. Mayor Kearns greeted the businessmen coming out of church with a real election-day smile after giving his wife a loving squeeze on the arm that turned her pale.

I felt sorry for Mrs. Kearns. Suddenly I wanted to go up and hug her and kick Mr. Kearns in the shins, but I couldn't tell you why.

When Grandfather and I talked after church he said that Mayor Kearns' face was like the headlights of a car. His Honor could turn it on whenever he wanted to light up a useful patch of road, or he could turn it off whenever he wanted to hide a secret shortcut.

"What kind of a secret shortcut?" I asked.

"To put it delicately," Grandfather answered, "Mayor Kearns is a slippery crook."

Of course, everybody in our town knew that my grandfather was death on politicians. Actually, he was *sudden* death on politicians, the clergy, and the government—all three, and in no particular order.

"Too many of them are more interested in the fleece than they are in the flock," Grandfather said.

Unfortunately, Grandfather said those things in public, and as often as he could, so there were a lot of places in Green Valley where he wasn't too popular. In fact, there were quite a few places where he was not even welcome—such as the town hall meetings where Grandfather challenged the speakers with troublesome questions like "Why are we paying five hundred dollars every year to paint three bridges that we never built with the fifty thousand dollars the state gave us to build them fifteen years ago?"

Or like the time he asked at a revival meeting, "*How* is Christ going to come down on a cloud? Clouds don't come *down*, they go *up*. They're vapors that rise from the earth. And if Christ *did* come down on a cloud—which He couldn't—He would have to make several million solo flights before everyone in the world could see Him, and 'most everybody sitting here at this revival meeting would be dead before He landed in our neck of the woods!"

"These kinds of questions don't make you any friends with the party in power," Grandfather told me, "but they might make people think. They just might."

He laughed, tickled me until I nearly fell over, and

admitted, "Of course, they haven't been thinking for several hundred years, but I like to give them the benefit of the doubt."

Another place where my grandfather wasn't always welcome was in my own house, but only when he talked about priests, ministers, politicians, the government, doctors, or the church. This didn't leave Grandfather much room to talk when he came to dinner because most of the things he felt like saying were on the forbidden-subjects list. Grandfather usually found some sly way to slip into one of these subjects from left field. He certainly livened things up until once, when my mother nearly fainted, and he was sent home in disgrace.

"It's their disgrace, not mine," Grandfather had insisted as they shoved him out the front door.

I don't think people really tried to understand what my grandfather was talking about. I don't think they listened. Whenever Grandfather started in, everybody felt he was attacking them personally, and all they did was fight back.

Actually, Grandfather told me there were politicians who loved and served the people. "They're statesmen," he said. "The priests and ministers who love God and obey His laws are spiritual giants. And the doctors who are more interested in taking out your bad gallbladder than your wallet are angels of mercy."

"Then why are you so mad at everybody, Grandfather?"

"I'm after the rotten apples," he told me. "Trouble is, everybody's got some secret thing they're ashamed of, so they always think I'm after that, and they get their backs up. Pity."

7

Actually, I intended to tell the story of how I committed a sacrilege and fell in love with Angela Raffodil in church, but so far it's been mostly about crooks and vipers, and there hasn't been much love in my story at all.

Maybe that's what makes love so important: it's so hard to find any of the real stuff. I thought everybody loved *everybody* until I was nearly seven years old. Then I had my eyes opened. By the time I was ten I was nobody's fool.

2

Angela, Millicent, and Lucille

Anyway, Father O'Malley certainly stirred up a hornet's nest with his sermon about the whited sepulcher. It had pleased everybody, even the two Winthrop girls, because everybody thought they knew exactly who Father O'Malley was talking about, too.

"We sure seem to have a lot of whited sepulchers in our town," I told Jimmy Middleman.

"My old man said it's that bootlegger who's been watering down his stuff."

That's when I heard the Winthrop girls giggle. Everybody called them the Winthrop girls, although they were both as old as the town cannon. Their names were Millicent and Lucille. Grandfather said their names sounded like an opera. Apparently their lives were just as tragic as an opera, too, because everybody referred to them as "the poor Winthrop girls."

They had all kinds of money, so I knew they must be

poor for some other reason. You could tell they had suffered just by looking at them. Millicent and Lucille were all wrinkled up like a couple of plums that had been left out all summer on a hot tin roof.

When you went to the Winthrop house to deliver packages, the girls never answered the doorbell. First, they came and peeked out through the lace curtains, one at a time, with one head appearing above the other. It was creepy. Calling them "girls" made me feel creepy, too. (I was still in grade school.) And Mayor Kearns said the Winthrop girls should have died of old age years ago. He had started saying it right after the Winthrop girls stopped contributing to his campaign fund.

I knew how the mayor felt. Both Millicent and Lucille were cheap tippers. I never got more than one cent for doing them favors. And I mean one single copper penny. I never knew which one was Millicent and which one was Lucille because they not only looked alike, they sounded alike, and they both always said the same thing, often at the same time. They'd take the parcel you'd delivered right out of your hands, and then one of them would hold out a penny and say: "Here's a bright, shiny, new penny for a very nice boy!"

Often it was a dirty penny at that.

It was Millicent and Lucille Winthrop who brought Angela Raffodil and me together, so I never thought of them again as the *poor* Winthrop girls. Angela and I both sang in the choir. Angela was a contralto and stood between Gabby Daniels and me. I was a tenor, and he was a baritone.

Gabby was a boy who never talked unless you asked him something, and, since his answers were never very good, I never asked him anything. But apparently Angela did. Some people said they had a thing together. Angela looked up at Gabby on her right side and down at me on her left, although Angela wasn't much taller than I was. She was about as much taller than I as she was shorter than Gabby. That left me with the short end of the stick.

Gabby was a sophomore in high school and played football. He didn't have to say much as long as he kept making touchdowns. About the only thing Gabby and I had in common was Angela. Of course, neither Gabby nor Angela realized that.

One winter the three of us had the flu at the same time. When the poor Winthrop girls were next to come down with the flu and needed someone from the choir to take a basket of food to them, the three of us were sent. We were the only ones who were already immune, and I was the only one who knew exactly where the Winthrop girls lived.

The Winthrop girls didn't open the door when we knocked, but they did peek out from behind the curtains. Their faces were ghastly. Their eyes looked like wet Concord grapes on white plates.

Gabby took one look and said, "I think they died and sent their ghosts back."

"This hot soup'll get cold!" I shouted. But they didn't answer. The curtains closed, and no matter how loud we knocked and hollered, the Winthrop girls refused to reappear.

Gabby Daniels whispered to Angela, "I wonder if Doc Kelly treats them out here on the doorstep?"

Angela laughed. Her laughter sounded more beautiful than when the whole choir hits the "Ave" in "Ave Maria."

"Maybe Doc Kelly gives them their injections through the keyhole," I suggested.

Angela giggled and said, "William!" trying to sound shocked, but I knew I'd hit her funnybone.

Gabby didn't like playing second fiddle on the funny stuff, so he tried to get rid of me. He patted me on the back and said that he and Angela could take care of things now, and why didn't I run along. Angela wouldn't hear of it, though. She said the three of us should stick together. And we did. For exactly the ten minutes it took Angela and Gabby to walk me home.

I tried my funny line again. "Do you suppose Doc Kelly gives the poor Winthrop sisters their injections through the keyhole?"

Angela didn't laugh. That's when I noticed that she was already half a block away, walking along, holding hands with Gabby.

Angela Raffodil and I spent a lot of time together that year while she was refusing to go to picnics, parties, and the movies with me. Angela didn't say I was too young for her, but she did say I was too short for going to the movies and things out in public. But Angela always made me feel that tomorrow was another day and that I might suddenly tower over her. "Tomorrow is another day" was one of her favorite expressions.

So far, tomorrow was always just another day, I was still too short, and Angela still said no, but I wasn't in any hurry. I didn't have anywhere else to go.

❖ ❖ ❖

One afternoon I came down to my grandfather's barn while he was greasing the wheels on the harness-racing sulky.

"What do you suppose is wrong with me?" I asked him.

"Do you want a list?"

"I'm serious."

"Likewise."

"Did you ever stop to realize, Grandfather, that all through grade school I've been mostly interested in girls whose names begin with the letter *A?*"

My grandfather told me, "I haven't lost any sleep over it."

"It's true just the same!"

"So?"

"So I'm worried. For a couple of years now, I've been mixed up with girls named Amy Kimball, Annabelle Thomas, and now Angela Raffodil. They're all *A* girls."

"Maybe you're working your way through the alphabet."

"Of course," I said, "there *was* Lois LeSarde, and, off and on, Margie Kelly."

"That saves it."

I could see that Grandfather wasn't impressed with any of this. Usually he had some helpful suggestions for a fellow when he was faced with a serious problem. I told him so.

Grandfather stopped greasing the sulky long enough to say, "I don't shoot rabbits with an elephant gun."

I was peeved. "Okay, so it's *not* World War II. I'm still worried about whether I like Angela because she's Angela, or because she's got a name that begins with the letter *A.*"

"Why don't you make calf-eyes at a girl whose name begins with the letter *B* and then study your reactions? Maybe you can just taper off the *A*'s."

There was no use talking to my grandfather when

his mind was on trotters or pacers, so I went up to the house to find my sister, Ella. There wasn't much use in talking to Ella at any time, but on a gloomy Sunday you are sometimes forced to scratch around in barren gravel.

"I've got a real mystery here, Ella," I said.

"Get lost!" she said with her usual tenderness.

"I've noticed that all the girls who are crazy about me this year have names that begin with the letter *A*. What do you make of that?"

"It means that *A* stands for 'asinine.'"

"I'm wondering if I should stay away from girls whose names begin with the letter *A?*"

Ella gave me a scathing look. "Until you grow taller than a baseball bat, no girl is going to be crazy about you. What you mean is that you're crazy about them, and you don't care what initial their names begin with. If you mean Angela Raffodil," Ella shrilled disdainfully, "why, she doesn't even know the color of your eyes."

I knew right then that I was never going to be in love with any girl whose name began with the letter *E*. Also, I didn't believe a word Ella said.

I managed to meet Angela Raffodil later that day. It was about two o'clock. I watched her house from the concrete block factory, and when she came out, I followed her uptown to Sweetman's Ice Cream Parlor. I stopped her when she came out.

"I want you to do me a favor," I said.

"You're too short," she said.

"This'll only take a minute."

"The ice cream will melt."

"Turn your back to me."

Angela did.

"Now say the first thing that comes into your mind when I ask you this question. Ready?"

Angela didn't answer, so I turned around and saw that she was already about twenty feet down the street. I hollered after her, "What color eyes do I have?"

She hollered back, "Who cares? Whatever color they are, I wish you'd keep them off me for a while."

I made believe that my back was still turned, and I counted off the ten paces you're supposed to take when you're fighting a deadly duel. Only I let it run to about fifty paces, then I turned the corner for home.

I decided that maybe my sister Ella might know more about the Winthrop girls than she did about the alphabet. When I got home I asked her what terrible thing had happened to the poor Winthrop girls to turn them into curtain peekers.

"Get lost!" she told me.

"I've got a right to know."

"You asked for it." Ella looked around carefully, then spelled it out for me. "S-E-X," she whispered.

It was obvious that my sister Ella didn't know anything, so I tried Father. He was reading the Sunday paper. I had to cough three times before he put down the sports section. He took off his glasses, lowered his head, sighed, and said:

"I'm all ears."

I told him, "I've been trying to figure out why they call Millicent and Lucille 'the poor Winthrop girls.' I know they're rich, so there must be some secret reason. I've been trying to find out all through grade school."

Father said, "Wait until you're in high school."

"Ella says it's sex."

Father called to Mother. "Ethel! Get your daughter Ella in here."

This, I thought, should liven up Ella's Sunday.

It didn't. In some mysterious way, my sister Ella came off with flying colors, and I got the hairbrush. If Kaiser Wilhelm could have bottled my sister Ella, he'd have won the war.

I decided that the only sensible thing to do was to ask the Winthrop girls themselves why everybody called them that. It took me nearly a week to get them away from the curtains and out onto the doorstep. They were quite cheerful when I asked my question. They smiled and patted me on the head. "Here's a bright, shiny, new penny for a very nice boy," they said in unison. "Perhaps you'd like to buy a sack of jellybeans."

With a penny? I could see that it had been a long time since the Winthrop girls had bought any jellybeans. They were obviously way out of touch with the modern world.

The strange thing was, I liked Millicent and Lucille. They were ancient, and I didn't like calling them "the poor Winthrop girls," or even "girls." They had been girls when Jesse James robbed the Glendale train. I suppose I liked the Winthrop girls the way you like a robin with a busted wing or a cat with the colic.

When the Winthrop girls smiled, it was a weak and puny thing. Even when they laughed, there was no fire or fun in it. That's why I was so happy to hear them giggle and laugh right out loud when they came out of church on that Sunday morning when Father O'Malley preached his whited sepulcher sermon.

Millicent hugged her sister's arm in sheer delight.

"It was sweet of Father O'Malley to try to disguise it, but the moment he mentioned whited sepulchers, I knew at once that he was talking about—"

"Shhhh!" Lucille warned. But she, too, could hardly suppress her joy.

This was the first time Millicent and Lucille Winthrop had come out of their house in almost five years. They had said they wanted to welcome the new priest to the parish, and they felt certain that his message had been exclusively for their ears.

"Isn't it heavenly?" Millicent cried. "That dreadful woman! At last! She's finally getting her comeuppance!"

I leaned so far over toward the Winthrop girls to learn who that dreadful woman was, that I nearly fell over onto the sidewalk. Father O'Malley had set the town on its ear. I knew I had to find out the truth. *Somebody* must know who the whited sepulcher really was. I didn't place too much faith in Millicent and Lucille. I had learned from hiding behind the sofa when Mother entertained the Altar Society at our house that a "dreadful" woman could be anybody who didn't happen to be in the room at the time.

I stopped Angela when she came out of church. Maybe she knew who the whited sepulcher was. "I've got something to ask you," I said. "Something serious."

"Tomorrow," she suggested, "is another day."

"It's not about asking you for a date."

Just then, Gabby Daniels came out and joined us. He pried my fingers loose from Angela's arm and said cheerfully, "You'd better keep your eye on business, tenor. You were a little flat on that last 'hallelujah.'"

I had a good answer for that, too, but, considering the difference in our sizes, I decided to forget it.

Anyway, there was no reason for Gabby Daniels to bend my thumb way back like that.

I figured there was only one place I could go to get an answer to my question about the whited sepulcher. That was down at my grandfather's barn, sitting on the oats box.

"This one," I told myself, "needs an elephant gun."

3

Hell Is a Burned-Out
Volcano

I met Saphead Phillips on the way to my grandfather's
barn. He was as puzzled as I was.

"My father said the whited sepulcher was his foreman, Jack Garvey, but my mother said he was out of his
mind. She said that anyone with half an eye could see that
it was the snotty new librarian from St. Cloud with her
sheer silk stockings and her—that's when my old man hit
me on the ear with the Sunday paper and told me to beat
it."

"Chances are that the whited sepulcher isn't a Catholic at all," I told Saphead. He agreed.

"Probably one of the Lutherans in the white church
on Elm Street."

That made sense.

"Or one of the Holy Rollers in the shingled shack
down by the river," I suggested. "I'm on my way down to
ask my grandfather. He'll know."

"What if he's the whited sepulcher?"

"Then he'll tell us."

Grandfather knew everything about everybody in Green Valley. People told him things because he was so easy to talk to. Unfortunately, he had a bit of a mean streak in him. He wouldn't tell you what the people told him. Grandfather insisted that gossip and backbiting were worse crimes than murder.

"When people realize that man has a soul," Grandfather explained, "and that it's the most important part of him, they'll begin to understand. Murder only kills the body, Son. Gossip is more deadly. It kills a man's spirit, the everlasting part of him."

"You're sure a pretty talker, Grandfather," I told him.

"I know."

"You should have been a priest."

"You're right. But so far your grandmother, seventeen grandchildren, and a sense of humor have held me back."

"Besides, you're not even a Catholic."

"That's true."

"So what are you, then, Grandfather? A Protestant?"

"Well, I do like to protest a little now and then."

"But you're not a Methodist like Grandmother."

Grandfather chuckled. "Nobody," he said, "is a Methodist quite like your grandmother."

"You must be *something*."

"If I told folks in this town what my religion really was, they'd probably ride me out of town on a rail."

"Really? Is that why everybody says you're a radical?"

Grandfather laughed.

"A radical," he said, "is just somebody who doesn't believe the same things you do. Green Valley is rotten with radicals, only they all think they're conservatives."

"Father says you're an atheist."

"A 'dirty atheist,' I believe, is the way your father usually puts it. But he doesn't mean it. The trouble is, I kind of like everybody's religion. Did you know that the Greeks called Socrates an atheist because he believed in only one God?"

"I never even wanted to know it," I told him. "Besides, I know you're not an atheist. You're a much bigger God-talker than Father. He gets nervous."

"He's worried about his immortal soul and things like heaven and hell and sin."

"Aren't you?"

"Nope. To me, Son, heaven is just a lovely place of blue sky, and hell is a burned-out volcano."

"What about the devil?"

"You mean that clever fellow with the horns, the long tail, and the spear?"

"That's the one, all right."

"If I tell you what's happened to the poor old weatherbeaten misfit, who won't you pass the news on to?"

I answered in a flash. "F-A-T-H-E-R."

"Good. Then we'll take that up next Sunday."

"You always quit at the best part," I objected.

"You might pass on that tip to Father O'Malley."

My grandfather was one of the few people in our town who wasn't afraid to talk about the devil in unfriendly terms. Mr. Einar Olson, who was a fundamentalist, believed that the devil not only existed, but that he overheard everything you said. That's why Mr. Olson never comes to visit my grandfather anymore—not since the day Grandfather challenged the devil to a fair fight, with Mr. Olson looking on. Mr. Olson almost died of fright right there in Grandfather's barn.

Grandfather and Mr. Olson were arguing about whether the devil really existed. When my grandfather made one or two very uncomplimentary remarks about the Prince of Darkness, Mr. Olson turned white. He looked like a man who'd had his blood drained out down to the kneecaps.

"Quiet!" he warned. "The devil is listening to every word. He'll punish you!"

Grandfather cackled delightedly.

"You're sure the devil is listening?"

"Positive!"

"Good!"

Grandfather got up off the oats box and stomped on the ground with his good leg and beat on it with his cane. "Can you hear me down there, Devil? If you can, come up out of there and face me like a man! You no-good, sidewinding, two-horned sneak! I say you're a yellow-bellied troublemaker! If you dare show your face around my barn, I'll kick the living daylights out of you! So come up here and face me like a man! Otherwise, you can go to hell!"

Mr. Olson ran screaming from the barn, while my grandfather laughed until his sides hurt. I was amazed. I pointed to the floor.

"You mean there's really no devil down there at all?"

Grandfather shook his head. "Not now, there's not."

"Where is he?"

"Who do you think was chasing Einar Olson?"

"The real devil?"

Grandfather ruffled my hair. "The devil's imaginary," he said. "He's inside all of us, unless we kick him out. But he's only in our imaginations. I'll explain it in more detail when we have more time."

No devil?

"This is going to take some getting used to," I told Grandfather. "I've been trying to get the devil to put a curse on Sam Raffodil for two years now. No wonder I haven't been getting any results."

❖ ❖ ❖

I told my father and mother at dinner that night that there was no hell.

Father laughed. "If there's no hell, then where has business gone to?" he wanted to know.

Mother said, "That's not funny, Frank."

When I told them that not only was there no hell, but that there was no devil in charge of operations there either, no matter what anybody told you, Father agreed with Mother that it wasn't funny.

Father was very broad-minded. He accepted all of the doctrines of the Church for his family, even if he wasn't crazy about them himself.

My sister Ella said, "He's been talking to Grandfather again. Everybody but Grandfather knows there's a hell. It says right in the Apostle's Creed, 'He descended into hell, and on the third day He arose from the dead!' If there's no hell," Ella asked me, "what was He doing down there for three days?"

"Don't ask me," I told her. "Maybe he was looking for the place, couldn't find it, and finally gave up."

My father snapped, "That's enough, William."

"Yes, sir."

"You know you are forbidden to discuss the Church or the clergy with your grandfather."

"The Church and the clergy, yes, but Grandfather said that the devil was in the public domain, so it would be all right."

"Your grandfather is wrong."

"Yes, sir."

Mother went to the telephone and called Grandfather.

"What have you been telling this boy about hell and the devil?"

Mother listened for a moment and then hung up.

"Well," Father asked. "What did the old reprobate have to say for himself?"

"I must have gotten a wrong number," Mother told him. "Somebody with a Chinese accent answered the phone."

I laughed to myself because I knew that whenever my grandfather didn't want to get involved on the telephone, he answered in a singsong Chinese voice. There was a lot of my sister Ella in Grandfather.

Father telephoned the next time, but by then my grandfather was conveniently out on Tamarack Road with the horse and buggy and couldn't be reached.

Grandfather told me that one of my grave weaknesses was a very big mouth.

4

Buckshot Thorne against the Stars

I always enjoyed the things that my grandfather taught me. Sometimes they caused me a lot of trouble, but usually it was worth it. And I never turned beet red in the face when I talked with my grandfather like Mayor Kearns, or Doctor Kelly, or my father did. I asked Grandfather why that was. He said it was because I listened and hadn't already decided what he meant before he started talking.

"People are like cameras," Grandfather told me. "If the picture they've got inside them is already exposed and developed, there's nothing that can change it. No matter how much light you may shine in there, it doesn't do a thing but light up the same old picture. But, if people would crank up their camera to the next negative film on the roll and let in a little sunlight of truth, they might get an entirely new picture."

I don't want you to think that my grandfather didn't have any friends. He did. Quite a few friends. But most of them were people who were in trouble with other people.

My grandfather had a lot of friends like Buckshot Thorne, although Grandfather said he was more of a refuge for people like Buckshot Thorne than he was a friend. Grandfather said Buckshot's problem was that he thought of himself as a man who was frank and outspoken when, in truth, Buckshot Thorne was really just plain rude. If you judged Buckshot Thorne by the way he acted, you wouldn't like him. If you judged him by the way he thought about himself, you might have been a little more charitable. Nobody liked him.

"What you have to do is try to judge a man on what he means inside, not what he does outside," Grandfather explained. "Most of the people in the world are outside judgers. That's why it leads to so much bloodshed."

Buckshot Thorne was the blacksmith in our town. He was also the man who took up the collection each Sunday in our church. Buckshot made up from memory a list of what all the people in our church were contributing each Sunday. If Buckshot Thorne hadn't read the list out loud one night at a church card party, I don't think old Mrs. d'Angelo would have resigned from the church. Grandfather said that being drunk was no excuse for Buckshot Thorne's behavior, even though it was on stolen altar wine. For just a "maybe Protestant," my Grandfather sure seemed to have a lot of Catholic information.

Mrs. d'Angelo was the richest woman in our church. She was also a widow who kept saying that she was going to donate her entire estate to a girls' school when she died. But Mrs. d'Angelo just kept getting healthier and richer. A lot of the girls who had hoped to go to her school grew up, got married, and had children who hoped to go to her school, until they grew up and got married, too. Not that anybody wanted Mrs. d'Angelo to die right away or anything. It was just that she was taking her own sweet time about it. Mrs. d'Angelo prided herself on her generosity and charity. At least she talked a lot about it. Nobody seemed to know exactly what Mrs. d'Angelo had ever given to anybody, nor could they find anybody who had actually gotten anything from her. There was just a lot of talk from Mrs. d'Angelo about bountiful gifts going out in all directions. My grandfather said it was one of those rare cases of "where there's smoke," there's no fire.

Maybe that's why Buckshot Thorne's revelation caused so much trouble that night at the card party when he announced in a very drunken voice that old Mrs. d'Angelo had been putting only a quarter in the collection box every Sunday for the past fifteen years. Mrs. d'Angelo never came to our church again.

Most of the parish was very upset. They felt that the Lord would be a lot better off with fewer Buckshot Thornes and a lot more Mrs. d'Angelos. Grandfather said that God would have to make that decision, not the Lady's Aid Society.

"But she was a pillar of the church." I said. "Mother said Mrs. d'Angelo was a mighty oak tree."

"Maybe they shook out too many of her acorns," Grandfather replied.

I happen to know that Buckshot Thorne gave five dollars to the collection every Sunday, and he was a poor man. Maybe he got tired of having the Lord let Mrs. d'Angelo get all of the publicity when He wasn't getting any of her money. Buckshot Thorne said he wasn't accusing Mrs. d'Angelo of being stingy. He just felt that she was one of those rich people talked about in the Bible, only, in her case, she could go through the eye of a needle a lot more easily than a camel and could take along all of her quarters without touching either side. This didn't do much toward getting him back into Mrs. d'Angelo's good graces.

Grandfather said that Mrs. d'Angelo couldn't have been too deeply rooted in her faith if Buckshot Thorne could drive her away that easily from the Lord.

"When the hurricane blows," Grandfather said, "the mighty oak trees fall, but the lowly grass bends and bows before the wind."

"Whatever that means," I said.

I think the reason everybody in Green Valley was so annoyed was not so much that the Lord was losing Mrs. d'Angelo as it was that the Lord's servants were about to lose Mrs. d'Angelo's four-hundred-acre estate. Mrs. d'Angelo gave her land and buildings to an old man from Brainerd named Joshua Jacobs who had started a Far-Seeing Foundation there. People said it was an institute for the study of the stars and planets, with a little palm reading thrown in on the side. In no time the whole estate belonged to *Father* Joshua, as Mr. Jacobs liked to be called.

Father Joshua wasn't really anybody's father—at least not like Father O'Malley was. Actually, Father O'Malley wasn't anybody's father, either, but Mr. Jacobs wasn't even anybody's brother.

Mrs. d'Angelo took up the study of the stars instead of the church. She threw herself into it with reckless abandon. Buckshot Thorne said it was because the stars were a lot farther away from the collection plate than the church was. Buckshot Thorne was drunk again at another card party when he said that. Mrs. d'Angelo announced that Buckshot Thorne was dangerously balanced on the cusp of Saturn, not to mention being in the worst possible house of Uranus. Buckshot Thorne said he had an answer for that last crack, too, but it wasn't decent enough for mixed company. But Buckshot did offer to tell Mrs. d'Angelo privately.

Father Joshua Jacobs claimed that he could read the future and said that, unless Buckshot Thorne kept his mouth shut, his future was very, very dark indeed. Grandfather said that if Mr. Jacobs could read the future, he probably kept his own bags packed, too. Grandfather told me, "I personally know that when Joshua Jacobs went deer hunting last winter, he was lost for three days in the woods, even though he had a compass and clear skies. So I wouldn't count too heavily on his reading the future when he's having that much trouble with the present."

The trouble between Mrs. d'Angelo and Buckshot Thorne grew to become one of the most famous religious feuds of our town. Everybody heard all the news as soon as it happened because both Buckshot Thorne and Mrs. d'Angelo were good friends with our postmistress, Gladys Tidings, and Gladys was friends with everybody, even the people she didn't like. I guess you have to be if you want to hold a job with the post office. "That's politics," Grandfather said.

Whenever Buckshot Thorne or Mrs. d'Angelo would tell Gladys Tidings the latest development in their feud, Gladys would spread it all over town from the post office. Gladys Tidings could give you the latest gossip from Hill City to Little Falls before you finished licking a two-cent stamp. Although her name was Gladys, people called her "Glad" Tidings, even though most of the stuff she told people was pretty sad.

Mrs. d'Angelo had been the organist in our church before she left the fold. She'd played all the music for our choir, and that's how Angela Raffodil and I both knew Mrs. d'Angelo so well.

One day I followed Angela Raffodil from her house all the way downtown—from the opposite side of the street, of course. When she went into Potter and Casey's store, I went around the block and came in the other way so I could have a peek at her through the household goods. I was pretty sure Angela would still tell me "Tomorrow is another day," but at least I could admire her from a distance today.

Mrs. d'Angelo was in the store when I got there. She saw me, she saw Angela, and then waved to us. Before we realized what we were doing, both Angela and I said, "Hello, Mrs. d'Angelo."

Angela looked like she was more surprised to see me than she was to see Mrs. d'Angelo. I, myself, was very startled by the appearance of Mrs. d'Angelo. She was the first person I'd ever seen who had been excommunicated from the church. Grandfather told me it meant "kicked out."

With Mrs. d'Angelo losing her soul like that, I expected to see a woman all shriveled up and shrunken. But when Angela and I saw Mrs. d'Angelo in Potter and Casey's, she still looked pretty good. I guess it hadn't gotten to her yet.

Mrs. d'Angelo gave us a quarter. "For a special treat," she said.

Figuring that a quarter was as much as Mrs. d'Angelo ever gave the church in one whack, I was surprised. Angela and I hurried away together as fast as we could. We breathed a lot easier once we got outside in the fresh air.

I told Angela that fate always seemed to be bringing the two of us together, and that maybe "tomorrow" had come, and could we go to the Saturday church supper together?

"No," Angela said, "no church supper, but we had better get rid of the tainted money that Mrs. d'Angelo gave us."

We decided to have ice-cream sodas at Nick the Greek's. We didn't tell him about the quarter's being tainted. Nick went to the Greek Orthodox church in the next town, so we figured he probably wouldn't have worried about it anyway.

That was my first date with Angela—I mean, where we were out in public together. It was a pity it had to be financed with excommunicated money, but I was happy to be breaking the ice with Angela in any way that I could. I was making so much noise motorboating the last of the ice cream up from the bottom of the soda glass with my straws that I didn't hear Angela get up from the table. When I saw that nickel in change come sliding across the table toward me, I looked up. Angela smiled and told me to keep it.

The sun was shining through her hair, and her eyes were so blue and big that, for a moment, I forgot about getting the very last bit at the bottom of my glass. One of the things I liked best about Angela Raffodil was that she didn't do any strange things with her eyes when she talked to you. She didn't bat her eyes like Margie Kelly did, or balloon her eyeballs out like fat Lois Lesarde. Angela Raffodil just used her eyes for eyes. She was the most natural person you'd ever want to meet—just as friendly and natural as a boy. But don't let that fool you. Angela was a girl, all right. Wow! Was she something!

I told Grandfather that Angela and I had eaten up Mrs. d'Angelo's tainted money, except for the nickel change, which was Greek Orthodox and not Catholic, so it was probably all right to keep it.

"I feel kind of sorry for old Mrs. d'Angelo," I told Grandfather. "She's going to burn in hell for mortal sin forever and ever."

"Don't let it keep you awake nights," Grandfather said. "They're developing a lot of new spiritual asbestos these days."

5

Discovered!
The Whited Sepulcher!

I'd have drowned myself in the Mississippi River if I had
realized anybody knew that I hung around after church
every Sunday just so I could look at Angela Raffodil. When
the fellows wanted to play baseball, I told them that I had
to wait around church for my old man. That was always
safe. My father came shooting out of St. James Church
every Sunday like a bullet, so nobody ever knew that he
was already out of sight. In fact, my father could be home
reading the sports page while the altar boys were still putting out the candles.

I needed a lot of excuses for hanging around the
church every Sunday. It's pretty hard to make believe that
you have important business on the church steps for longer
than fifteen minutes at a time. Of course, you can always
tie your shoelaces or even take off one shoe and shake out
imaginary stones. But after a while you run out of likely-
looking stuff to do.

First thing you know, people are beginning to give you the eye. I was just starting to feel conspicuous when I saw Angela come running down the steps to join her father and mother.

Wow! Was she something!

I'm not going to try to describe Angela any more than I did when we were at Nick the Greek's. In the first place, you'd think I was lying. I've made a few foolish exaggerations in my time over some pretty ordinary-looking girls like Margie Kelly and fat Lois LeSarde. Alongside Angela, they were leftovers. Just imagine the prettiest girl you ever knew, then forget her. She's a crow alongside a bluebird. You could have used Angela's face on the cover of any magazine, and you'd want to throw away the magazine and keep the cover. Have you got the picture?

Angela had the same name as her mother, Angela, just like Sam Raffodil had the same name as his father, Sam. It was a good thing Mr. and Mrs. Raffodil didn't have any other children, because they didn't have any other names.

But, let me tell you—they didn't need anything besides Angela. Wow! Was she something!

Funny, how you can live in the same town with the same girl for years and years and never think of her as anything but an ordinary good friend and never even apologize when you bump into her at school. Then, suddenly, she shucks off her cocoon and comes out a butterfly!

Let me tell you another thing. Angela Raffodil was welcome to light in my buttercups any time of the day or night, if that's where butterflies light.

It was a pity that Angela was Sam Raffodil's sister. That was the only thing against her. Angela was as beautiful as Sam was ugly. She was as nice as Sam was miserable—which made Angela just about perfect.

The first time I had really noticed Angela Raffodil was during choir practice the previous year. Mr. Harrison, the choir director, was trying to locate the sour note among the tenors during "Sweet Mother of Perpetual Help." Angela knew it was me, but she didn't let on. A lot of the tenor and alto section was below par that day because of the caramels fat Lois LeSarde had given out. The next time I noticed Angela was about ten minutes later when she was chewing on her caramel during the intermission.

Fat Lois LeSarde was sloshing hers around in her mouth like a wet mop in a bucket. Margie Kelly was noisy, too. Her jaw was going up and down as if she were trying to beat the caramel to death. Angela, on the other hand, was nibbling with the sweetest little rabbit-like bites you ever saw. I knew then that somebody had cast me a lovely pearl in the midst of these other swine.

The third time I noticed Angela was the following Saturday. I was hauling a load of manure in the buckboard for Grandfather, so I couldn't very well offer her a lift. When I came down Maple Street, Angela Raffodil was standing in her front yard in the middle of millions and millions of different-colored hollyhocks. When Angela waved to me, something inside me churned up so strong that I just kept kicking the front of the wagon until I got a hangnail on my big toe and limped for a week.

I have to admit that I was somewhat stirred up earlier in the summer by the hot kisser from Apple Bluff, fat Lois LeSarde, and by the Hill City woodcutter, Annabelle Thomas, and even by my next-door neighbor, freckle-faced Margie Kelly. But none of them were like Angela! Never!

That's the trouble with the English language. You have to use the same old words over and over for something that's entirely different. And Angela was that, all right!

I guess the truth is that a lot of girls start coming out of their cocoons and caterpillar skins in the summertime, almost like a plague of locusts. It's all luck which bug bites you. I can't honestly say that I minded. The only thing I want to make clear is that none of the other girls was ever like Angela Raffodil. I don't want you to think that this was just a weakness in me.

I talked with a lot of Amys, Annabelles, Margies, and Loises later in life, and they told me, to my horror, that at a time when I was absolutely positive I was their one and only flame, they didn't even know that I was alive. While I found these revelations a little troubling, they didn't come as a complete surprise. Even back in those days I was a little concerned, and I can remember asking my grandfather why nobody else seemed to realize how important the relationship between Angela Raffodil and me was—not even Angela Raffodil.

"That's because most of us are geocentric, instead of heliocentric, people," Grandfather explained.

"Thanks a lot," I told him. "That nails it right down for me."

Grandfather sat me down on the oats box to explain it. He liked to show off how much he read. Grandfather especially liked it if you appeared ignorant. I could help him out there without much trouble.

"For years," Grandfather explained, "people thought the earth was the center of everything and that the sun circled around us. That's geocentric, earth-centered. Actually, the sun is the center of everything in the solar system, and all of us revolve around the sun. That's heliocentric, sun-centered. Got it?"

"I've got it, but I don't want it. It doesn't have anything to do with Angela Raffodil!"

"It has everything to do with her. You think the whole world revolves around your life and your association with Angela Raffodil. It doesn't. You may be just another planet circling around Angela, and maybe not even a very important one at that."

This was pretty rotten news to me, but plain enough so I could understand it. "You mean it's just too bad if somebody is stealing a lot of geese in St. Paul, but if somebody steals my pet goose, Gog, right here in Green Valley, I'll scream bloody murder for the sheriff?"

"Well," Grandfather replied, "I won't say that's exactly the Ptolemaic or Copernican theory, but I think you've caught the spirit of it."

"You mean everybody thinks he's the most important person in the whole world?"

"Give that boy a big cigar!"

"And that's bad?"

"It's pretty much what's wrong with the world—nations, races, and religions, too. They're self-centered instead of God-centered."

Sometimes my grandfather could give you too much of a good thing. I didn't mind talking about Angela Raffodil, but I didn't have the stomach for races and religions.

❖ ❖ ❖

The Sunday of Father O'Malley's famous "whited sepulcher" sermon, I was sitting on a branch of the big maple tree by the church, waiting for Angela to walk by with her mother. I don't care what anybody's theories say. It isn't every girl who can make you want to climb up a maple tree in public and in broad daylight.

After Angela walked by, I must have fallen out of the tree. I was daydreaming, I guess. I didn't even remember walking up and down across every stack of pinewood in the Dow Lumber Yard, but I must have because, suddenly, there I was at my grandfather's barn. I had thought I was still up in the maple tree.

My pet goose, Gog, flew up and sat on my head, and I never said "hello"—not even when he pecked my ear.

Grandfather looked up from his work when I walked right into the barn door without opening it.

"Been to church, I see," he said.

"How did you know?"

"By the lovesick, moonstruck, vacuum-headed, simpering appearance your face takes on every time you shinny up that maple tree to spy on Angela Raffodil."

"I *never!*"

"That's where you were sitting when I drove by in the buggy."

"I never saw you."

"Of course you didn't. I whistled at you and offered you a lift, but you were in a trance. Your eyes were standing out like two peeled hard-boiled eggs. I'm surprised you didn't fall out of the tree."

"I did."

"From the look on your face, you must have fallen on your head."

"But I wasn't spying on Angela Raffodil. I was up in the maple tree for reasons of my own. Personal reasons."

"Well, then, I'm sorry," he said. "It being daylight and all, and with so many people around, it never occurred to me that you'd climbed up into the privacy of the maple tree to ease yourself. Naturally, I thought—"

"Grandfather!" I was shocked. I could feel myself turn the color of the inside of a stuffed olive. Grandfather looked at me with supreme innocence.

"What's the matter?"

"That's vulgar!"

Grandfather shook his head.

"I'm damned if you don't sound more like your mother every day. Look," he said patiently, "the ways of nature are not the mysteries of the pyramids. If you're going to run into the broom closet every time somebody yells 'bloomers,' you'll spend the rest of your life spying from up in maple trees. Don't be vulgar, but don't be a prude, either. Climb down from that tree like a man, look Angela Raffodil right in the eye, and invite her for another soda. I can't say that I blame you any."

"You—you like Angela?"

Grandfather said, "Wow! Is she ever something!"

I was alarmed. I had never breathed a word of that private expression about Angela Raffodil to another living soul. "What did you say, Grandfather?"

Grandfather chuckled. "That's what you said in your sleep the other night."

I was outraged. "Talk about spying!"

"Don't be so prickly," he said. "You asked to come and spend the night with me. I didn't invite you. Besides, these 'Angela things' happen to all of us sooner or later. You're just an early starter."

"I don't know what you're talking about."

It was a lie, and he knew it.

"You can't put strings on a rose bush and pull it up into full bloom," Grandfather said. "You've got to gentle it along slowly, with love. Let the sun and the rain fall on it in season. You've got to protect the plant from the bugs and from the weather. Let the rose grow naturally in its own time."

Grandfather patted me on the back. "That," he said, "is what I'm trying to do with you."

"Are you talking about Angela Raffodil?"

Grandfather nodded. "And Margie Kelly, and bulgy Lois LeSarde."

"Fat Lois LeSarde," I corrected.

"Amen!"

Then I remembered what Jimmy Middleman and I had planned to ask Grandfather the first chance we got.

"I've got a problem," I told him.

"Oh?"

"About whited sepulchers."

"You planning to play in the cemetery?"

"No, sir."

"Then you're not likely to stumble over any whited sepulchers unless you trip on some of the live ones we've got walking along Main Street."

"Is that what a sepulcher is? A grave?"

Grandfather turned and looked closely at me. "You must have had a cheery Sunday up there at St. James," he said, grinning.

I told him about Father O'Malley's sermon.

Grandfather laughed out loud. "No better way to make friends with the whole parish in one day."

"I've just caught on," I said happily. "The whited sepulcher may not be the mayor at all. It could be Sam Raffodil, Jr., just like I thought. It's a dirty old grave; that's what it is—something painted pretty on the outside while everything's dead and rotten on the inside."

"Welcome to Green Valley," Grandfather said, giving me a cuff on the head. "Present company excepted, of course."

6

Fire! Fire!
Turn the Hose on Me!

When school began that September, it was a turning point in my life. The very first day of school they gave us new lockers.

"Hot dog!" I told Jimmy Middleman. "We've got lockers right next to each other."

"You're crazy," Jimmy said. "I'm way around the corner."

"Not *you*—her!"

"Her who?"

"Angela, stupid. I'm 191, and she's 292."

"But 292 is up on the next floor."

"I know that, but it's right next to mine. I mean, if it were on this floor, it would be."

"What's so wonderful about that?"

"Don't you *see?* I can go up there and make believe I got there by mistake, having the number right next door and everything."

"But everybody knows that Angela Raffodil's

homeroom is on the second floor and yours is on the first. She's going to graduate this year. You're still a punk."

Jimmy was right, although he had a rotten way of expressing it. You can only pull that "I'm sorry, I must have made a mistake" stuff once or twice. After that, they get wise to you. And if somebody like Gabby Daniels, who had locker 291, tells you to "pull your freight," you can't keep hanging around waiting for Angela.

However, I got in some pretty decent Angela-watching from up in the maple tree at church, and, during the recess periods, I could look at her from behind the slides. Twice I walked behind Angela and followed her home from only half a block off. Once I pulled right up to within fifty feet.

Angela lived in the opposite direction from me, over in "Snob Town," which was not exactly on my way home, but I didn't have anything better to do. In fact, nothing half as good.

One Saturday afternoon at the movie theater, I met Angela face to face at the ticket booth. I'd been trying to arrange it for three weeks. I knew Angela went to the movies every Saturday. Even at that, I had to wait twenty minutes behind the meat-market truck to time it just right. Angela and I actually bumped shoulders as we bought our tickets. I admit that I leaned a little. I apologized profusely. "I'm sorry, I didn't see you standing there."

"Hello, William," Angela said. "Well, it looks like we are finally going to the movies together after all, doesn't it?"

Angela laughed.

"That's great!" I told her.

"Would you like to join me?" she asked.

"Would I!"

Wow! Was she something else!

Then I saw Sam Raffodil, fat Lois LeSarde, and Margie Kelly waiting at the door. It was a blow, but I weathered it. I glanced at Margie Kelly, then at Lois LeSarde, but my heart had already passed them by without a moment's hesitation. It's a big handicap for cabbages when they wind up in the same row with a perfect peach. It was hard for me to believe that I had once been madly in love with each of these girls. Now I had no more feeling for them than the wind does when it blows on your cheek in the summer.

I had thought it was fairly pleasant to look at the faces of Lois LeSarde and Margie Kelly until my eyes moved over them that day at the theater, and I compared them to Angela. When I looked into those two beautiful, blue pools on Angela Raffodil's face— ping! Just like that, I went from purgatory to paradise. I dove into the pool and went down for the third time, not caring if I ever came up. Margie Kelly and Lois LeSarde died the death of a rag doll, right there before my eyes.

But that Angela! Wow! Was she something!

I began to whistle out loud as I walked down the aisle behind her. I was already figuring out ways I could maneuver around Sam so I could sit beside Angela. I sang the words of the song to myself:

> I'm burning up! I'm burning up!
> Fire! Fire! Fire!
> Turn the hose on me!

From that moment on I knew that maple trees, school

slides, and walking behind were out. This was the real, close-up stuff. What a school term it was going to be!

I wondered just how much of this a guy could stand.

I could see that Angela wanted to find a seat where it was darker and more private. She passed the balcony lights and went down into the darkest part of the theater. I felt a shiver of excitement go up and down my spine as I followed her into the seats. When we sat down, I was right next to her. I had shoulder-shoved Sam a little for position, but it wasn't my fault that he stuck his ice-cream cone in the usher's ear. Sam got rapped on the knuckles with a flashlight in return.

Margie Kelly sat on my other side. Then came fat Lois LeSarde. Sam sat on the aisle so his injured knuckles wouldn't bleed on Lois.

Real wealth in this world, according to my grandfather, is not what you can accumulate for yourself, but what you can get along without. I learned that bitter lesson there in the dark theater that Saturday afternoon. I heard Angela Raffodil giggle happily and thought it was because of me.

"Can I hold your hand?" she whispered.

"Can you!" I said, thrilled.

I figured that in the dark theater I must look older and taller to Angela. I took a moment to wipe the caramel off on my trouser leg and then held my hand out to her. I was nearly sick with ecstasy.

When Angela ignored my hand, I leaned over and saw the terrible thing that was taking place. Angela wasn't talking to me, she was talking to somebody in the other seat next to her. It was Gabby Daniels!

"Hello, Tenor," he said.

"Hello, Baritone," I answered.

That's the way we greeted each other when we met at choir practice.

"It's very sweet of you to help me this way, William," Angela said. Then she confided the whole awful truth to me. "My father doesn't want me to go out with boys yet, so I told him I was going to the movies with Sam and some of his friends. That way Gabby and I can meet here secretly in the dark."

The way she said "Gabby" and "in the dark" made me feel like somebody had stuck a sword right through my innards.

Margie Kelly dug into me with her elbow.

"Isn't it thrilling!" she trilled. "They're in love!"

When Angela Raffodil and Gabby Daniels began to hold hands right in front of my eyes, it was like seeing my whole world going up in flames. I could hardly watch the movie. Her words had said, "Ready! Aim! Fire!" and I was executed without even a blindfold over my eyes. I kept turning the other way so I wouldn't see Angela and Gabby holding hands. I had to watch Charlie Chaplin with only one eye.

Margie Kelly was caught up in the romantic atmosphere, I guess, and she took hold of my right hand. I let her get stuck up a bit with caramel before jerking it away.

"If you want some popcorn," I said, "take it. But don't claw me. I hate hand-holding."

Angela leaned over and offered me half of her candy bar. "Are you enjoying the movie, William?" she asked.

"Great!" I told her. "It's simply great!"

"You're a real friend."

"You bet," I told her.

Right then I knew that the whited sepulcher was me—me, myself, and I. I was lying. I didn't think the movie was great at all. I was trying to make myself look good on the outside, while inside I was all rotten.

"I love my fellow man all right," I told myself with a hollow laugh. "It's just my friends that I hate."

Grandfather says that every man should live so that if his tombstone could talk, it wouldn't say, "This man is a liar!"

At that moment mine would have said it.

I told everybody I was going out for more popcorn, but I went right out of the theater and headed for home. To take my mind off the wretched way my love affair had turned out, I walked like Charlie Chaplin for two whole blocks. The rest of the way home I walked with one foot on the curb and the other in the gutter.

I kept dropping kernels of popcorn every now and then so the Secret Service could follow my trail and find my body before it was too cold.

47

7

Bless Me, Father, for I Have Sinned— Or Have I?

My grandfather had practically saved my life several years earlier when I was getting ready for my first communion. It wasn't the first communion that troubled me. What nearly polished me off was the first confession. We had to confess all of our sins so we could be purified before we took communion.

I spent a whole week trying to think of something halfway decent to confess. Later on in life, it was quite easy. Then it became a process of weeding out the unimportant stuff. But that first confession really had me stumped. That's why I took the problem down to the oats box in my grandfather's barn.

"I'm in trouble," I told him.

Grandfather kept right on sewing up the harness he was working on. "Do you mind," he asked me, "if I don't fall down with astonishment? Man was born to trouble as the sparks fly upward. You, particularly."

"I need some sins," I told him, "for my first confession. Some pretty big ones."

"Sit on the oats box."

We sat there in silence for so long I thought Grandfather was stumped for a solution. That worried me. Grandfather had never been stumped before. "So you need some sins," he finally said.

"Yes, sir."

"Well, I suppose I could let you borrow a few of mine, to sort of break the ice. We could really open up Father O'Malley's eyes with one or two of those."

"I'm a little young for any *really* big sins, don't you think, Grandfather?"

"I thought you said you wanted some pretty big ones."

"Sure, but not big enough to put me in jail or anything."

"Well, then," Grandfather said, "what we want are some sins that will satisfy Father O'Malley but won't trouble the authorities. Is that about right?"

"Yes, sir."

Grandfather put a new hole in Beauty's harness because she was getting fat from the soft life with him. Then he started working on my problem in earnest. "I suppose murder is out, then," he said. "A little too rich for starters anyway."

"Out," I agreed.

"Besides," Grandfather said, "there's no one we dislike that much, is there?"

I shook my head. "Nobody."

"Well, there's always horse-stealing, although that's

not as popular as it used to be."

"I need something smaller," I said. "Much smaller."

"Tell you what we might do," Grandfather suggested. "We might bag a gunnysack full of Mrs. Casey's chickens after dark tonight. We could return them after you go to confession. That way you'd have a sin but still would have a way out unless, of course, we were to decide to roast one of the plumpest."

I turned down that suggestion, too. One after another, I had to refuse all of my grandfather's ideas. I got the feeling that Grandfather wasn't taking my request for some sins seriously enough.

Finally he told me, "Son, you'd better just tell Father O'Malley that you haven't done anything that needs confessing. I'm sure he and the church will be able to stand up under it."

"I couldn't do that," I told him.

"Why not?"

"All the other kids have got plenty of sins."

"How do you know?"

"They've been talking about it. They've got some beauts."

"Such as?"

"They won't say. They just roll their eyes out of sight and say, 'Wait'll I get in there!'"

Then I had a great idea. "Why can't I just confess some of the things I *didn't* do?"

"For instance?"

"Well, I won a prayer book and a rosary for knowing the Seven Deadly Sins and all of the Ten Commandments by heart. I could use them and say, 'Bless me, Father, for I have not sinned. I haven't any strange gods before me. I didn't covet my neighbor's wife. I didn't commit adultery. I didn't—.'"

"Hold the phone!" Grandfather didn't look too pleased. "You're not supposed to brag," he said. "You're supposed to get the guilty things off your conscience. There may be a little good therapy in confession, but not until you've actually got something to confess."

"But I've got to confess something. Father O'Malley expects it. I don't want to be a failure."

"Let's sleep on it," Grandfather said.

8

Horse-Stealing
vs.
A Gunnysack of Chickens

We did sleep on it. And neither of us came up with anything useful, right up to the moment when I was standing in line along the wall by the confessional in St. James Church.

There were fifty-three of us in alphabetical order by our last names. Since my initial was *S*, I was almost the last one in line. Artie Armilla was first. Jimmy Middleman sneaked out of line and pushed in beside me. He looked sort of green.

"I can't think of anything," he said.

"Don't look at me," I told him. "I've got my own troubles."

"Can't you think of anything, either?"

I didn't enjoy the idea of being thought of as someone who had never sinned in his whole life, so I tried to give Jimmy the impression that Father O'Malley would have his hands full with me.

"I'm trying to weed out the small ones," I told him. "That's my problem."

"How about loaning me a few?"

I offered Jimmy my grandfather's assortment of murder, horse-stealing, and a gunnysack full of Mrs. Casey's chickens, but Jimmy wasn't buying any of them either.

"Murder!" he shouted.

Everybody in the church turned around to stare at us. I told Jimmy to hold it down if he wanted my help.

"Well, golleee," he whispered, "I want Father O'Malley to give me absolution, not Extreme Unction."

During all this time Artie Armilla still hadn't come out of the confessional. Both Jimmy and I began to get worried.

"For gosh sakes!" Jimmy said. "What do you suppose Artie could've done?"

"Search me," I told him. "He always seemed like a nice kid to me."

"He's from Minneapolis, you know," Jimmy whispered. "You can get into a lot more trouble in the Twin Cities."

When Artie finally came out, we looked at him suspiciously. He didn't look any different, but he certainly didn't look like it had done him a world of good either. Artie could tell that we were suspicious of him because of the long time he'd been in there. He smiled kind of sickly and said, "I lost my marbles."

He looked like he had, too.

"I mean, on the floor. They fell out of my pocket, and I couldn't find them."

Jimmy nudged me and said, "I've lost my marbles, too, and I haven't even gone in there yet."

Sam Raffodil popped in next. He was back out in no time. I leaned over and whispered to Jimmy, "He's a liar!"

When Jimmy came out of the confessional, he passed directly in front of me. Jimmy didn't say anything, but he rolled his eyes right out of sight, which didn't help build up my confidence.

Finally there was no one in front of me. I was the next sinner on deck, as they say in baseball.

George Shelby nudged me from behind.

"Get in there, Stupid," he said.

So I parted the curtains and went in to the side of the confessional that was closest to me. There were three compartments, and Father O'Malley was sitting in the middle compartment, waiting for me, or so I thought. Someone else would go to the other compartment on the other side.

I didn't find out until later that, just before I entered, Father O'Malley had received a phone call and had returned to the parish house. I waited a long time. I kept thinking to myself that whoever was on the other side of the confessional must certainly be a humdinger. My classmates went up in my estimation a long way during that first confession. Whoever was on the other side made Artie Armilla look like Mother Goose. I tried to figure out alphabetically who could be in there from the other line.

As the minutes went by, I began to have a little more respect for a gunnysack full of chickens, horse-stealing, and, toward the end, even for murder. My own stuff seemed awfully puny next to whatever the "hip, hip, hooray" sinner on the other side of the confessional had done.

I waited and waited. Eventually, I had the horrible thought that maybe Father O'Malley had been in there all the time, waiting for me to begin, although I had heard his reputation wasn't built on patience.

Cautiously, I leaned toward the latticework that Father O'Malley and I were to talk through and gently whispered, "Hello? Hello? Anybody in there?"

There was no reply.

As my eyes became accustomed to the dark, I could see that there was a closed shutter in front of me so I wouldn't hear the confession of the person on the other side. However, I poked an exploratory finger through the latticework to make sure. Just as I did, the screen was suddenly snapped up, almost severing my finger. I saw the shadow of Father O'Malley, and I nearly jumped right out of the confessional.

Actually, right then and there, I committed my first sin. I took the name of the Lord in vain. George Shelby told me so later on. He said I could be heard halfway down the church. I could see Father O'Malley's dim outline through the screen. He had a handkerchief covering the side of his face toward me. I'd forgotten who was supposed to start, but impatient noises from inside put me on the right track.

"Bless me, Father, for I have sinned," I began. "It's been nearly eight years since my last confession."

Father O'Malley grunted. "This is your first confession, isn't it?"

"Yes, Father. Really. But I'm nearly eight years old, and I was thinking of original sin, and I wanted to clear up the whole thing in one sitting. My grandfather told me about original sin. He said this sin was probably the only

shell I had in my rifle. Grandfather said that there was
nothing really original about original sin in his opinion—"

Father O'Malley cut me off and brought me back to
the business at hand. "This is not a place for reminiscences
about your grandfather," he said. "Get on with your confession."

"Yes, sir."

"Well?"

"I can't think of anything important, Father."

"Try something of lesser importance."

"I did. All week. I couldn't think of anything."

"Do you remember your catechism instructions for
first communion?"

"I remember the instructions, all right, Father. I just
can't remember any sins."

"Search your conscience."

"I have. I've been searching all week."

"Did you honor your father and mother?"

"I'll say! I wouldn't dare not to. My father, especially.
Golly, he says—"

"Just make a dignified confession. It's not necessary
to go into details."

"Yes, Father."

There was a long pause.

"But I can't think of anything else, even without details."

"Try."

"I've been trying all week."

"You said that."

"Yes, Father. Even my grandfather tried to think of
some sins for me."

Father O'Malley made some strange noises that I always associated with storm signals, so I apologized.

"If I'd known what was expected of me, I might have done better, Father. Maybe if I could have another week, I could figure out something to do and do it, so it wouldn't be a waste of your time."

9

Bad Bookkeeping
in Heaven

I realized later in life that Father O'Malley must have been
a noble human being. His reputation *was* built on patience,
after all. Getting the sins out of those young seeds was like
Doc Jensen pulling teeth with rubber pincers.

What's more, Father O'Malley heard first confessions
in four separate towns in that one month. I'm sure that
when he died, he went right into the Kingdom.

He nearly went into the Kingdom during that one
first confession we shared together. I could tell by the sounds
that were coming from inside the confessional that it wasn't
going according to the set plan we'd studied at Sunday
school.

I was never sure that Father O'Malley had lowered
the handkerchief and peered at me with one eye, but a
very uncomfortable feeling came over me until whatever
it was that was bright and shiny there in the dark disap-
peared again.

After a long sigh, Father O'Malley prompted me once more. "Have you ever taken the name of the Lord in vain?"

"What's 'in vain'?"

Father O'Malley sighed again. There was light pain in it. He cleared his throat. "You *did* attend the preparatory classes, didn't you?"

"Yes, Father."

"Have you ever used the holy name of the Lord carelessly?"

"I guess I did that all right, Father," I said, relieved that I had done something.

Father O'Malley seemed pleased. At last we were getting somewhere.

"How often?"

"Pretty often."

"How many times?"

"Quite a few."

"Can you be more specific?"

"What's specific?"

"Five times?" Father O'Malley asked.

"More times than that, Father."

"Fifty times?"

"Oh, no! Not that many!" I was shocked.

"Perhaps twenty times?"

"Somewhere around there."

"Shall we say twenty?"

"Let's," I agreed fervently.

I got up to go, but Father O'Malley lowered the handkerchief again. This time I could see that it really was a big shiny eye looking right at me. I knew I'd better not fool around. This was a place for sinners, not failures like me. I even considered throwing in horse-stealing so it wouldn't sound too pitiful. In the back of my mind, I was still worried about taking the name of the Lord in vain twenty times. I told Father O'Malley so.

"Suppose it's more than twenty times, Father. I'd be lying to the Lord."

"Twenty times *approximately*," Father O'Malley explained patiently, or almost patiently.

I was still worried.

"What about the Recording Angel in heaven that Sister Aurelia keeps telling us about in school—the Angel who keeps everything written down in black and white, word for word, and who doesn't miss a thing?"

Father O'Malley's voice took on that tone that everyone in the catechism class had learned to recognize as a warning that it was crisis time.

"You may set your mind at rest," he told me. "The Recording Angel will make the necessary adjustments. You have my word. Now get on with it. This is a solemn sacrament, my son, not a debating society."

"Yes, Father."

I still remember how Father O'Malley's whisper filled the confessional. It had a low, rich, rolling rumble to it. Father O'Malley went way up in my estimation, but the Recording Angel went way down. I told Jimmy Middleman about it later, and we agreed it was pretty sloppy bookkeeping up there. After that, whenever Sister Aurelia would mention the Recording Angel, Jimmy and I would slyly wink at each other, knowing that the necessary adjustments were being made in heaven.

I stopped daydreaming long enough to answer Father O'Malley's question, which he had repeated several times. "Have you cursed?"

"Yes, sir, Father. I mean, I did swear a few times here and there. Just little stuff. Not like my father. Golly, when he lets loose—"

"How many times?"

"Quite a few."

Father O'Malley sighed. "Approximately?"

From bitter experience, I suggested, "Shall we say twenty times?"

I honestly think Father O'Malley said, "Let's," but it was hard to tell because he sounded like he was sorry he had come. Father O'Malley waited for me to go on with my sins, but I still couldn't think of anything worthwhile. I realized that I was a pitiful specimen. All the sins I'd talked about so far had come from Father O'Malley. I felt ashamed, and I knew that Father O'Malley must be disappointed in me, too. His big sigh filled the inside of the confessional and blew his handkerchief straight out from his nose like a flag in high wind.

"Have you stolen?"

"What?"

"Anything?"

"How recently?"

"Since the day you were born."

"I can't remember that far back."

Father O'Malley's voice began to take on a little edge. He sounded more Irish than usual. Every student in St. James Sunday School knew what that meant, too. Run for the hills!

"Can you remember anything at all about the classes we held to help you make this first confession?"

"Only the Bishop catching me with his shepherd's

crook if I miss any catechism questions when I'm confirmed."

"You won't be confirmed for some time," Father O'Malley explained. His voice sounded like he doubted that I would ever be.

After a long, long pause, Father O'Malley seemed to summon up all his resources to go on. "Is there anything else? Anything at all?"

I realized right then and there that I'd been wasting Father O'Malley's valuable time with my "damns" and "hells," "little white lies," and "more or lesses." I felt pretty sick about the whole thing. I decided that God would understand my problem a lot better than Father O'Malley, so I came right out with one of Grandfather's suggestions.

"Well, I stole a gunnysack full of Mrs. Casey's chickens after dark."

Father O'Malley came to life.

10

The Confessional Beats the Woodshed

Apparently it can be quite exiting in the confessional if you have something to deliver. I could tell that Father O'Malley thought I'd been stalling all this time because I'd been too ashamed to admit to stealing Mrs. Casey's chickens.

"How many times?" he asked.

I was alarmed.

"Well, not twenty times, I'll tell you that! Not even approximately."

I was sorry now that I'd ever mentioned chickens and the gunnysack. I began to think of how sacred it was to go to confession, and I was sorry I'd told a big lie. It was just that I wanted to have something decent to confess like everybody else. Something worthwhile. Otherwise, there didn't seem to be much reason to be there at all.

"Did you return the chickens?"

"No, Father. Actually, Father, there weren't any chickens in the gunnysack."

"What was in the gunnysack?"

"Actually, Father, there wasn't any gunnysack, either."

Father O'Malley glanced toward the other side of the confessional as though he wished he could get on with some plain, ordinary "taking of the Lord's name in vain."

"It was my grandfather's idea," I told him. "He just made that up as a sin I could use if I felt I needed it."

"Then your grandfather is the one who should be going to confession."

"He's not a Catholic."

"Pity."

Then Father O'Malley began to ask me about all the other things I should have remembered to confess. I guess he figured the only way to get me out of there was to lead me by the nose. It wasn't so bad after all. There were quite a few things I'd done. Most of them, I have to admit, were "approximatelys" and "somewhere around there, Fathers," but at least I began to feel better about the whole thing. In fact, by the time we were through, I was almost proud of myself.

I did have to remind Father O'Malley about one thing. "We didn't settle about the stealing, Father," I said. "I don't want that on my conscience."

"Did you steal?"

"Not the chickens, but maybe you could call it stealing."

"It's quite simple," Father O'Malley explained. "Did you take something that didn't belong to you?"

"In that case, I guess I did steal."

"What?"

"I took it from my next-door neighbor last Fourth of July when he was eating dinner."

"What did you steal?"

"A balloon."

There was a long, pregnant pause. And when I say pregnant, I mean like triplets or quadruplets. Then Father O'Malley finally said, "For your penance say five Our Fathers and five Hail Marys. Now make a good act of contrition."

"Father—"

"That's all."

"But there's something that I should—"

"That," Father O'Malley said, "is *all.*"

He didn't spell "A-L-L," but his voice did.

"I've forgotten exactly how the act of contrition goes, Father," I said.

Right then I couldn't even remember the Ten Commandments.

"Do your best."

I finally said a Hail Mary sort of mumblingly so Father O'Malley might think I'd remembered the act of contrition after all. I knew it all right, but I was too nervous to remember how it started. I could say it walking along the street like blazes, but inside that confessional I was hopeless.

I told God I was sorry about the gunnysack and the chickens just before Father O'Malley shut the lattice screen. When he banged it down, I jumped right out through the curtain.

My first confession was over!

I was absolved from all my sins, and I knew that sometime later on I'd probably feel pretty good about it.

I had waited inside the confessional for over fifteen minutes while Father O'Malley was taking his phone call, and with my own confession on top of that, I'd been in there almost a semester.

George Shelby gave me a fishy look as I came out. He looked down at his wristwatch and up at me. Then he whistled softly under his breath. You could tell that everyone still waiting in my line was making a mental note to keep a sharper eye on me from now on. A lot of general distrust spread through the ranks on that historic afternoon.

It had sure been embarrassing going to confession without anything worthwhile to confess that first time. It made me feel like there must be something wrong with the way I had been brought up. I promised myself that the next time I went in there, I'd have plenty to confess. But that first time I might just as well have stayed at home. In fact, I wished I had.

After a few months I didn't mind going to confession at all. I wasted no time. I had all my sins lined up and ready. I could get in and out nearly as quickly as Sam Raffodil, and without lying. I seldom got more than ten Our Fathers and ten Hail Marys. Once, though, I did get the stations of the cross from Father O'Malley. That was right after *someone* stole seven of Mr. Olson's ripe watermelons.

That same night I got fifteen lashes of the razor strap from my father in the woodshed. I decided that I preferred the confessional to the woodshed. In confession, God let you get it out gradually, of your own free will, and you could sort of make it sound better. My father, on the other hand, used an extra-long razor strap to beat it out of me, in juicy detail. Of course, you never had any penance at the end with Father, but before, during, and immediately after, it was like being fed to the lions.

I don't think the punishment would have been as bad

if my father had just taken down the razor strap and gotten right to work with it. His method was to keep the whole razor strap rolled up in a tight coil, holding it that way with his thumb. When the moment of truth arrived, Father would cluck his teeth, release his thumb, and the razor strap would slowly unroll down to its full, fierce length.

My father was a tooth-clucker of great dramatic ability. Unfortunately, he was also a just man. Mr. Middleman, Jimmy's father, on the other hand, was a merciful man. Jimmy could get away with murder.

The week I got the stations of the cross and the razor strap on the same day, I developed a very useful technique. I told the truth in the confessional, and I lied at home. It didn't seem right to suffer twice for the same thing. I asked Grandfather about this. He said it was double jeopardy. Even so, Grandfather was against lying in principle. He said that a man's whole life was a confessional. Sometimes my grandfather could make you wish you'd gone to the movies instead of down to his barn.

I found it very comforting to know that you could do just about whatever you wanted to, then unload the whole thing on Father O'Malley on Saturday nights and be ready to start out fresh again.

I also found that my father was wrong about something. You can't be excommunicated for pinching watermelons, even if you do it three or four times and sell them at a pretty decent profit.

Jimmy Middleman agreed with me. "That's what church is for," he said. "To give a fellow a second chance."

"Or a third?" I suggested.

Jimmy said "Amen!"

11

God's Pagan Bill Collector

As soon as my first confession was over, I went right down to the barn to see my grandfather. He was hitching up the team of dapple-grays.

"I'm purified," I told him.

He said, "Don't lose it."

Unfortunately, I did.

Happily, I kept my "goods" and "bads" balanced enough so that Father O'Malley let me serve mass after a few years went by. Father O'Malley usually teamed me up with Teddy Martin, who was nearly a saint.

Teddy dropped a lot of touchdown passes and was weak in the infield, but at the altar Teddy was an all-American.

Teddy pulled me out of trouble on more than one occasion—like when I fell asleep at early mass and forgot to ring the bells. Another time I brought the altar wine to the Epistle side instead of the Gospel side of the altar. I was trying to show off my profile so Angela Raffodil could see how handsome I looked from the front pew where she sat with her family. A sudden and loud *"Oremus* (Let us pray)" from Father O'Malley rattled me, and I shot up to the wrong side of the altar.

Sometimes I sang in the choir, sometimes I served mass, and sometimes I helped take up the collection. Father O'Malley thought it would be appealing to have young faces taking up the collection. It would be more likely to touch the heart, which would help touch the pocketbook. He felt it was a lot safer, too, ever since Buckshot Thorne had made up the list of what everybody was putting into the collection plate.

One Sunday I passed the collection plate to the pew where Mr. Raffodil was sitting. My eyes bugged right out when I saw him waving a five-dollar bill. Old Mr. Raffodil was as tight as the lug nuts on a Model-T Ford, and for him to give five whole dollars in one crack was like seeing stars fall from the sky and the moon turn into blood. Old Mr. Raffodil made certain that everybody else knew about it, too, by "harrumphing" and clearing his throat noisily before crumpling up the bill and tossing it nonchalantly into the collection plate.

The funny thing was that that five-dollar bill never showed up when we counted the collection. I searched the whole sacristy, even behind the altar wine. Jimmy Middleman and I even searched each other. There was no five-dollar bill.

The next Sunday, I changed sides with my pal, Jimmy. Jimmy nearly flipped the plate over when he saw old Mr. Raffodil wave another five-dollar bill. But we never found that five dollars when we counted the collection that day either. We didn't tell Father O'Malley about it because we thought he might think one of us took it.

I had some suspicion that Jimmy Middleman had taken it, and he had some suspicion that I had taken it, but we finally decided that old man Raffodil was palming the five-dollar bills and tossing in a one-dollar bill.

My father, however, tried to make sure nobody knew that he was putting a five-dollar bill in the collection plate. He just did it with the numbers folded back out of sight so nobody could see how much he was giving. Of course, my father only gave the five dollars once a year at midnight mass on Christmas. The rest of the year he nickel-and-dimed the Lord like everyone else.

Father O'Malley said he liked the Sunday collection the best when he couldn't hear a sound from the altar. That meant everybody was putting in paper. When he could hear the "clink, clink, clink," he knew the Lord would have to run his house on low-test.

I decided to tell Grandfather all about Mr. Raffodil and his vanishing five-dollar bills.

"You know I don't like gossip," I told him.

Grandfather snorted.

"And you taught me never to say anything about anybody unless it was good. And this *is* good!"

As I told the story, Grandfather chuckled from time to time, so I could tell he was amused by it.

When I'd finished, I told him, "Old man Raffodil is pretty much like his son, Sam. A real blister."

"That does seem a mite deceitful," Grandfather agreed. "I'll tell you what, Son. Let me think about it. Maybe I can figure out a way to get young Father O'Malley's money back."

"I've never heard of anybody having any luck getting money out of Mr. Raffodil," I told him.

"Ah!" Grandfather said. "But you are now dealing with a vintage sinner. I've traded horses with too many slippery customers to be stumped by a fellow skinflint like Sam Raffodil."

"You're really wonderful, Grandfather," I told him.

He chuckled. "Wicked, yes. Wonderful, no. But I do have a little hankering to milk that money back out of old Sam Raffodil. I owe him one. We'll see. We'll see."

Whenever my grandfather said, "We'll see," boy, would you really see, and I mean something spectacular! I wouldn't want to have been in old man Raffodil's shoes then for anything. I wouldn't have minded being in Sam, Junior's, shoes, though, since his mother had just gotten him some new beaded Indian moccasins. But that's another story.

My grandfather was true to his word. He did think of a way to bring Mr. Raffodil to justice. It happened at a big church social. Everybody in the parish was there. It was a benefit held by the Altar Society to take up a big collection for the new parochial school that was to be built.

Most of us went to Benjamin Franklin Public School. Father O'Malley had chosen three of us altar boys to give two-minute speeches on what a new parochial school would mean to us.

Grandfather had written my whole speech for me, and we practiced it together down at the barn. I stood up on the oats bin and delivered it to him several times. I had never heard him laugh so hard before. To me, it wasn't that funny a speech at all.

It began with a tribute to Mr. Sam Raffodil, Sr. That alone was enough to put me off. On the night of the big church social, I delivered my speech loudly and clearly in front of everybody.

"Beloved friends, I want to say right out loud what great happiness it gives me every Sunday when I help take up the collection. Every Sunday, I see Mr. Sam Raffodil, Sr., being so generous to Almighty God. A man like that can almost get the school built all by himself."

Everybody in the gymnasium turned to look at Mr. Raffodil. This wasn't the stingy Sam they knew. I went on bravely.

"Mr. Raffodil puts a big five-dollar bill into the collection plate every Sunday. He never fails. I've seen it with my own eyes. So has Jimmy Middleman. Both of us look forward to finding that five-dollar bill in the plate when we count the money after church."

Mrs. Raffodil, Angela, and Sam, Jr., were smiling proudly, but the old man looked like he'd just heard the judge say, "To be hanged by the neck until you are dead." I was almost afraid to go on.

"Mr. Raffodil never fails the Lord. Every Sunday, for two whole years that I know of, Mr. Raffodil has done the same generous thing. And when you add up all those five-dollar bills which Mr. Raffodil, Sr., has given to God, it comes to four hundred and fifteen dollars. I know that what we give is supposed to be a secret between ourselves and God and that I shouldn't be talking like this in public, but I'm sure that God looks down every Sunday on our church, and He must be very happy with what he sees Mr. Sam Raffodil, Sr., doing. And God sees every little thing there is to see, even a sparrow falling off the roof and breaking his neck. I think we should all give Mr. Sam Raffodil a nice hand."

Everybody did. But a lot of them did it reluctantly.

The applause was scattered and scant. I still thought it was a poor speech. I told my grandfather so, but he just chuckled and said, "There's a hidden rock in all that soft soap."

Maybe Grandfather was right. When the contributions were made that night, Mr. Raffodil sent up a check for $415.

Mr. Raffodil was very upset with me, though. He cornered me in the clothes closet after the meeting ended. He seized me by the collar and drew me close.

"I don't like my private affairs being bandied about in public," he said. "Especially by some young snot of a kid."

"Yes, sir."

"You had no business making up a speech like that."

"Oh, I didn't make it up," I told Mr. Raffodil. "My grandfather wrote it for me."

Mr. Raffodil was incensed.

"Why, that old pagan isn't even a Catholic! He isn't even a Christian!"

"Maybe not," I admitted, "but he's a good money collector. And maybe, like he says, God is his personal friend after all."

"I'll get even with the old devil if it's the last thing I do!" Mr. Raffodil promised. "You tell him that. I mean every word of it!"

I told Grandfather about it and about how purple Mr. Raffodil's face had been. Grandfather didn't break out into any sweat over it.

There was no five-dollar bill in Mr. Raffodil's hand the next Sunday when I passed the plate. He gave me such a look that I almost drew the plate back. I couldn't see anything but his clenched fist. Also, as I told Jimmy Middleman later, there was no rustling sound of paper money as he took his hand away. There was only a faint "clink."

"A five-cent clink?" Jimmy asked.

"More like a dime clink," I told him.

❖ ❖ ❖

I forgot all about my first confession until several years later, during the summer when we dedicated the new parochial school. Father O'Malley came back from Duluth for the occasion. Grandfather had been right. They had made Father O'Malley a bishop.

I met Father O'Malley on the street after the ceremonies. We walked together for a short way before I could make my getaway. Father O'Malley patted me on the head in a friendly way. "It's nice to see you again, William," he said. "I hope there haven't been any gunnysack burglaries since I went to Duluth."

I didn't know what he meant at first. Then it all came back to me with a rush—the gunnysack and Mrs. Casey's stolen chickens. I blushed all over. Father O'Malley was shaking with inner laughter. He shook like a bowl of Mother's best raspberry jelly. "But—but you're not supposed to know who's inside the confessional. It's a sacred, holy secret." I was horrified almost as much as I was ashamed.

"It is a secret. It most certainly is." Father O'Malley ruffed up my hair, then wiped the Vaseline off on his handkerchief. "It's still a sacred secret among the three of us. God, you, and your former parish priest."

"Golleee!"

"Over the years," Father O'Malley went on, "there

are some people who just stick in your memory, let us say. They stand out. Besides, there's only one grandfather of the gunnysack and stolen-chicken variety in Green Valley."

"Yes, Father."

"Good luck to you, Son," Father O'Malley said, turning into the parish house. "And, if you ever get into trouble, you know where to come."

I certainly did. And I made a solemn vow to myself that if I ever had to go to confession with Father O'Malley again, I'd disguise my voice.

12

The Blizzard of 1888
Was a Sun-Shower

The ice froze solid on Serpent Lake early in December and was followed by a blizzard that people nowadays wouldn't believe if you described it. Grandfather said he hadn't seen a storm like it since the year Grover Cleveland was defeated for president even though he had the most votes.

Grandfather knew when everything had happened the last time. If he didn't know, I suspected that he made it up. He said he always told the truth, except about horses, and even that was the truth as he saw it.

Grandfather also taught me to believe only one-tenth of what I heard and only half of what I saw with my own eyes. That's why I could look him straight in the eye when he said that about Grover Cleveland and say, "Yes, Grandfather," and say to myself inside, "Boy! Is that a lot of baloney!"

When I got home, I looked in the encyclopedia. It gave me a shock. I'm a son of a gun if the famous blizzard of 1888 didn't happen the year Grover Cleveland lost the presidency to Benjamin Harrison, even though Cleveland had received more popular votes. How do you like that old bugger of a grandfather? He could make ordinary facts sound like an exciting, interesting lie, and when you looked them up, they were the plain old truth.

I was in for another terrible shock during the week of our big snowstorm.

It sneaked down on us from Canada overnight. I'm not talking about an old-fashioned "white Christmas" snowstorm. I'm talking about a real blizzard.

For years I'd been listening to my grandfather talk about the big blizzard of '88. The wind picked up about five miles of speed per hour each year he told the story, and the snow grew thicker until it was no longer blinding, it was impenetrable.

I looked up the word "impenetrable" before I called Grandfather a liar. We were allowed to call each other certain names if we smiled. It was a gentleman's agreement. Grandfather insisted that he wasn't lying about the blizzard of '88. As time went on, he just remembered more and more of the details about it.

"I'm sick and tired of hearing about snow so thick you couldn't see your hand right in front of your face," I told him.

When Grandfather insisted that the blizzard of '88 was so bad that, no matter what color your skin was, you wouldn't be able to see your hand in front of your face, I broke our gentleman's agreement. I didn't even smile when I called him a liar. He took it in a pretty good spirit, outside of chasing me out of the barn with his cane.

I decided right then and there to prove that Grandfather was wrong. No blizzard had snow that thick, and my friend Jerry Haller, who was black, agreed to help me prove it. We had been waiting for three years to see if we would be able to see his hand in front of his face during a real blizzard, but all we had gotten were snowstorms—blinding snowstorms, all right, but no real blizzard stuff.

Then came that dark December day. That's what everyone in Green Valley called it: "That dark December day."

I've learned that grown-ups can't say simply, "Isn't this a nasty snowstorm?" or, "Wasn't that a dreadful accident?" They have to give it a special made-up name like "spine-chilling catastrophe" or "dark day." Anyway, it wasn't a dark day; it was a white day. If you stood in one place for over ten minutes, you became a snowman.

In just six hours Green Valley was covered all over with cold cotton batting. The whole town looked like a Christmas card. Our chimney had a ten-inch hat. You could slide down from our woodshed roof to the ground on barrel staves. I know because I tried it. It's true that my sister Ella had to dig me out twice. There was so much snow you couldn't tell where the woodshed roof began and the snow ended, except for the big holes I made.

People were snowed in everywhere. Wouldn't you know that it happened on the first day of the Christmas holidays? Of course, there was no guarantee that if it happened during a school week we would have been snowed out of school. We might have been snowed in with our principal, Mr. Edwards. He was pretty hard to take for just a few hours on a clear, sunny day, so maybe we were lucky after all.

You couldn't see your hand ten feet away. I know, because Jerry Haller came hurrying over to my house right away so we could try the scientific experiment we had been planning for years. We kept trying not to see each other's hands at different distances. Ten feet was about the shortest distance.

Jerry ended up being snowed in with me for three days. It caused quite a lot of excitement—not the blizzard, but Jerry's being snowed in at our house. A lot of the excitement took place right in my own kitchen. Mother didn't know Jerry was upstairs in my bedroom until it was too late for him to go home alone. She called me down into the kitchen. I told Jerry to peek down the hot-air register so he could see what was going on

"I've never entertained a Negro," Mother told me.

"You don't have to entertain Jerry," I told her. "We'll entertain ourselves."

"That's not exactly what I meant. Perhaps I'd better call his mother and see if she can't come and get Jerry before the storm gets too bad."

"She can't come."

"Why not?"

"She's dead." I was surprised. "Gee, you mean to tell me that in all the years the Hallers have lived here you didn't even know Jerry's mother was dead?"

"Then I'll call his father."

"He's away on business. Jerry's almost an orphan."

"Who does he stay with when his father's away?"

"His Aunt Rose. But she thinks he's upstairs in his bedroom studying."

"Then we'd better call her and let her know he's here. I'll telephone right away."

"They don't have a telephone. They're very poor. I thought we were poor until I went over to play at Jerry's house. We're rich."

"That's not the point, right now, is it?"

"No, ma'am."

"His Aunt Rose will be worried sick. And the day after tomorrow is Christmas day."

"Let him ride out the storm with me."

"How will Santa Claus find him?"

I gave my mother a look. We both knew that Santa Claus was my old man. "If there really is a Santa Claus," I told Mother, "and he can't find Jerry when he's a few blocks from home, then he'd better turn in his reindeer."

"I don't think you're getting the point."

"Besides," I explained, "Jerry says he's never had much from Santa Claus anyway. Certainly not enough to make it worth taking a chance on getting frozen stiff in a blizzard."

Mother was annoyed at something. She said, "Where do you pick up those outlandish expressions?"

"From Grandfather."

Mother told me to go back upstairs. She called Grandfather, told him what the problem was, and asked him to drive Jerry home. Grandfather was sitting by the potbellied stove in his parlor, playing cribbage solitaire. He said he wasn't going out into the storm for anybody.

"What am I going to do?" Mother asked him.

"Invite him for Christmas."

"But he's a Negro."

"You're lucky," Grandfather told her happily. "There's only one Negro family in town! You've got an exclusive."

13

There's No Entertaining Going On

Mother sighed, hung up the telephone, and went up to her bedroom to think things over. Jerry Haller sighed, too.

"She doesn't want me to stay, does she?"

"Why do you say that?"

"Lots of people don't. They don't say so. In fact, most of the time they say exactly the opposite, but you can feel it in the air."

"Not these people," I assured him.

Jerry got up from the window seat.

"I'd better start for home before the storm gets any worse."

"Okay, if you want. I'll go along with you. We can ride out the storm at your house."

"Your mother won't like that either."

"How do you know?"

"I just know. That's all."

I was annoyed. "I wish you wouldn't always be telling me how my mother's going to feel. I've spent a lot more time with her than you have. Are you going to help me settle this hand-in-front-of-your-face thing or not?"

"I guess so."

"Okay, then. Boy, you sure are a prejudiced person, Jerry," I told him.

He seemed surprised.

"Me? How come?"

"Don't ask me. All I know is that you're suspicious of every person in this whole town, and only some of them are suspicious of you."

Jerry could see that a scientific experiment was a lot more important than how a couple of relatives felt.

"All right," Jerry said. "Let's make another test."

We sneaked out my bedroom window and crawled out over the woodshed roof. You couldn't tell where the roof ended because it suddenly merged into a huge snow-drift. It was great! You couldn't even see the houses in front of your face—not until you crawled out of the drift, anyway.

It was becoming a real blizzard, all right. Fortunately I'd had a lot of experience getting around without seeing where I was going. And I don't mean stealing down in the dark at night to rob the icebox. I mean big-time blind stuff.

Once, when I laughed at the funny way a blind man stumbled over a big rock at the fairgrounds, Grandfather covered my eyes with some horse bandages and let me try doing my chores in the barn blindfolded.

"It'll be a good lesson for you," he said. "Most of us don't appreciate our eyes half enough." Grandfather laughed right out loud when I fell over the manure pile. "It's not much bigger than the rock," he told me.

Eventually Grandfather had to call off his experiment with me. I started to clean out Beauty's stall and accidentally pricked her in the hind leg with the pitchfork. She nearly kicked Grandfather into the next county. She also managed to knock out a plank in her stall, which knocked out a pane of glass in the window. After that, Grandfather said I'd been blind long enough, and he took the bandages off.

"It taught you a good lesson," he said philosophically, "and it won't cost me more than four dollars for a new window."

The good-natured pat on the back that Grandfather gave me knocked me into the oats bin.

When I told our club, the Mississippi Mudcats, about the blindfold experiment, everybody thought it was a terrific idea. We came up with the idea of a northern Minnesota blindman's bluff championship that very day. Whoever could travel all the way across town from the Soo depot to the Northern Pacific depot in the shortest time without peeking from behind his blindfold or knocking anything down would be crowned champion. We took turns being blindfolded.

The finale of the contest was set for Sunday afternoon, when there was usually little or no horse traffic. We all practiced for a whole week with only minor assorted damage. Unfortunately, the contest was called off on Saturday afternoon when Margie Kelly walked into the egg man, who was bringing the supplies for the church supper into her house. That was shortly after Saphead Phillips fell down the well in his backyard. Now you know one of the reasons why we call him Saphead.

Phil O'Brian didn't help matters, either. He tried

crossing town on his bicycle when the rules plainly said to walk. Phil rode into a construction site and went head first into a flat-box cement mixer. Only his big blindfold kept him from filling up his lungs with concrete. The foreman wanted to let the concrete dry on Phil so he could be placed in the town park as a statue of a real village idiot. That's when Phil got the blindfold off and started screaming bloody murder, so they ended up rinsing him off. All in all, the blindman's bluff championship wasn't a smash hit. Nobody's child was allowed to talk or play with me for a week.

Just the same, that professional experience at going around blind helped Jerry Haller and me get all the way across town to his house during the blizzard. We didn't go more than a few blocks out of our way.

Jerry's Aunt Rose didn't want me riding out the storm at their house any more than my mother wanted Jerry to stay at our house.

"Why not?" I asked Aunt Rose.

"I've never entertained a white person in my house," she said.

"I'll entertain him," Jerry told her.

I put my hat on. I said, "She doesn't want me to stay, does she?"

Jerry was pretty upset.

"This," he told his Aunt Rose, "is a scientific experiment. It doesn't have anything to do with entertainment."

We tried seeing Jerry's hand in the blizzard on their front porch, and, because it was easy to see at five feet, I figured it was safe enough to go back home.

Jerry's Aunt Rose wouldn't let me go back home alone, because the storm was getting worse.

"I'd better go to the corner drugstore and phone your mother that you're all right."

"Don't do that," I said.

"Why not?"

"She thinks we're upstairs in my bedroom. She might go into shock."

That's when Aunt Rose went into shock. She told Jerry to go back with me and to hurry, or we'd be caught in a blizzard worse than the blizzard of '88.

I lost Jerry once on Main Street. He lost me once by the Dow Lumber Yard. When we stopped for a rest under the town cannon in Lincoln Park, I said to Jerry, "You know something?"

"No. What?"

"The trouble with people is that nobody does any entertaining."

"You're right," he agreed.

It took superhuman effort for us to climb up the maple tree to the woodshed roof so we could get back into the house through my bedroom window. Jerry slid off the roof into the snowdrift once, and I did, too. Then we both did it because we liked it so much the first time.

Finally Jerry said, "We'd better get inside. The storm's getting much worse."

I knew he was right. I could hardly hear Jerry even though he was shouting and practically nibbling on my earlobe.

We finally made it inside. I crawled through my bedroom window first. Then I leaned out into the storm to help Jerry. I held out my arm.

"Gimme your hand!" I yelled.

"I am!"

I cried out, "I can't see it!"
Jerry said, "It's right in front of your face!"
Now, how do you like that?

14

The Ultimate Solution

Grandfather was right again!

That old rascal was right too often for comfort. It made me wonder if I'd been fair to him for thinking those evil thoughts on the occasions when I was sure he was telling me such terrible whoppers.

It was frightening to think that maybe all the things that Grandfather had been telling me all these years were true after all. It would make Grandfather a combination of Robin Hood, Billy the Kid, Samson, and a touch of Merlin the Magician. Even I wasn't prepared to believe that at first.

It's a pity you didn't know my grandfather. Maybe you could have sorted out the lies from the real stuff. Grandfather always admitted that he told a few fibs once in a while, but not on policy matters and only for dramatic color.

"A little classy lying," he called it. "Just so I won't look too good. It's embarrassing when the truth sounds more heroic than the lies. So I tone it down."

Jerry Haller and I hid our soaked clothes in my closet

so the snow could melt in peace where no one would notice it. Mother didn't even realize that we'd gone out.

My father stomped in from work just then. He kicked the snow from his shoes. He said the whole town looked like it was covered with marshmallow fluff.

"Everything," Father said, "is closed down tight and will be for some time. Nobody is going to be able to go anywhere for days."

Jerry whispered, "That means me, too."

"Great," I said. "Maybe we'll be stuck here together until summer vacation!"

Father made a profound statement.

"The snow is getting thicker by the minute. This storm is going to be worse than the blizzard of '88."

When Father walked past the big front window where Jerry and I were watching the storm, he said, "Hello, boys." Then he stopped dead in his tracks, turned around, and came back for another look. I could tell he was surprised at seeing Jerry Haller there with me.

"What's he doing here?" Father asked. "In this storm, I mean. Shouldn't he be home?"

I told him. "I thought it was time someone in this house entertained a black person. And when the storm stops, I'm going to his house so he can entertain a white person."

"He's going home right now," Father said. "His family is probably frantic. I'll call his father to come and get him."

"He can't come."

"Why not?"

"He's away on a trip."

"Then I'll call his mother."

"She's dead. Jerry's almost an orphan."

"Well *somebody* must be taking care of him."

"Somebody does."

"Who?"

"His Aunt Rose."

"I'll call her."

"She doesn't have a phone."

Father sighed. "Then I'll have to take Jerry home myself."

"Better not try," Mother said. "You won't be able to see your hand in front of your face."

"That's a fact!" I laughed. "Not even Jerry's hand. Grandfather was right about the blizzard of '88."

Father took a look out the window. The Baptist church across the street had vanished entirely. You couldn't even see the big oak tree by our front window.

"We should get word to his aunt somehow," he said.

"We did already," I told him. "Jerry and I walked over there and told her Jerry was here with me. We just got back."

"Why didn't Jerry stay home when he was already there?"

"His Aunt Rose was afraid I'd get lost coming home alone."

"Why didn't you stay there until I could come and get you?"

"His Aunt Rose was nervous. She'd never entertained a white person before."

When Mother found out that Jerry and I had been out in the worst of the blizzard, she was very upset. When she saw our wet shoes, she said we'd both have to go right upstairs and take a hot bath.

There was only enough hot water for one bath, so we

took a bath together. Was that Jerry Haller something to see lying against that white tub!

"Stand up and turn around," I told him. He did. "Hot dog! You're the same black color all over. You haven't got one white spot on you anywhere."

"I know it," Jerry laughed. "Ain't it great!"

Then I got up and turned around.

"Look at me," I said. "I'm white as the driven snow. What do you think of that?"

"You should eat more," Jerry said. "Your ribs stick out."

We splashed around until Mother came up and told us dinner was ready. While we were dressing, Jerry said, "I should have gone home alone."

"Why?"

"If you'd gone home alone from my place, the rescue party would never have found a paleface like you in all that white snow, but with me, at least, they'd have had a fifty-fifty chance."

Jerry said it was too bad more black people didn't live in the far north. People would begin to find out just how useful it was to have black skin in a blizzard. We both laughed at that, until we heard a scream that told us Mother had found our wet clothes in the closet. We were betrayed by the puddle of water running out from under the door.

Jerry Haller stayed at our house for three days and three nights. He was there until the storm broke. One morning we woke up, and the sun was shining. We had a great snowball fight before breakfast. It was Jerry and me against my three sisters and Margie Kelly.

Everybody got to know my friend Jerry really well during those three days. Mother said he was one of the sweetest boys she'd ever seen. That was laying it on a little thick, I thought, because anybody you're cooped up with for three days and three nights can be a pain in the neck, no matter what color they are. My sister Ella was a perfect example. But it does show you what a little entertaining can do.

When I told Grandfather about it, he was delighted. He said that maybe I'd uncovered the ultimate solution to the tragic racial situation in the country.

"What do you mean?" I asked.

Grandfather was intrigued with the idea. "If we could just get white people into half of the black homes, and the rest of the black people into white homes, and then come up with a helluva snowstorm, maybe we wouldn't be the laughingstock of the rest of the world."

15

Gimme That Old-Time Whitewash

Grandfather handed me the pitchfork and told me to go up into the loft and fork down some alfalfa for the horses. We hollered back and forth at each other as we talked again about Father O'Malley's sermon in detail and how everybody in town thought somebody else was the whited sepulcher. Father thought it was Sam Raffodil, Sr. Mayor Kearns thought it was Jebez Casey. And Jimmy Middleman thought it was the Protestants or maybe even Grandfather, himself.

"It is," he hollered up at me. Then he chuckled.

When I'd finished forking down the alfalfa, Grandfather told me to come down and sit on the oats box with him. "Let me tell you the fascinating story about the first time Pastor Andrews came to the Baptist church."

I'd heard the story dozens of times, but when Grandfather started a story, you knew you might as well listen to it cheerfully. If you told him you'd heard it, he'd say he left out a lot of mighty pertinent details the last time he told it to you. Trying to stop Grandfather from telling a story was like casting your trout fly into a stiff wind. It wound up back in your face and maybe with the point first.

The story was all about how Pastor Andrews would take each baby he baptized, hold it up, and stare at it as though he were overcome by the glorious sight. Pastor Andrews would say, "Now *there* is a baby!" That's all he ever said, but every mother reacted as if he'd called her baby the President of the United States or something. Of course it was a baby, because Pastor Andrews didn't baptize livestock. And, the truth is, most of the babies turned out pretty punk, or below average. Not one of them ever became famous, except maybe Salty Kramer. Salty was in all the papers before he went to the electric chair.

I sat there thinking sweet thoughts about Angela Raffodil until I could tell by the sound of Grandfather's voice that he was coming to the end of the story.

Then I asked him again, as though his story had never interrupted our conversation, "Which one of the people in our town is it? Really?"

"Which is what?"

"The whited sepulcher?"

"All of the people in town," Grandfather said. "Even you and me."

Grandfather arched an eyebrow, and I knew he was going to make a telling point. "When you lied about hiding up in the maple tree to stare at Angela Raffodil, it made you look good to yourself on the outside, but inside it made you feel like hell for lying, didn't it?"

I nodded. "Like hell."

Grandfather coughed. "Just grasp my meaning; don't repeat my words." Then, while he curried down Beauty, Grandfather told me confidentially that most people were like that. "There's not a manjack in all of Green Valley," Grandfather said, "who doesn't use the whitewash brush on himself whenever he can to make himself look good to other people."

"Even you, Grandfather?"

"I buy it by the hundred-pound sack."

Grandfather nudged Beauty. "Over, Beauty!" he said, and she danced aside to let him pass. Whenever Grandfather started addressing the horses before telling me something about life, I could be pretty sure it was going to be something good. So I was prepared for it.

"We're all whited sepulchers," Grandfather told me. "Off and on, like a basket of apples. We keep the red shiny ones on top and try to cover up the rotten ones underneath, or those with bad brown spots. We put the bright red ones up where people can see them, hoping they'll think our whole basket is like that and buy it. We hide the spotted ones, hoping nobody will notice. That's one of the values of psychology, son. You may think you're something pretty terrible, and it can worry you sick. Then, when you talk to the doctor, you find out that you're not the only one who has thoughts like that, and you feel you can go on a little longer."

"You mean everybody has bad thoughts?"

"Everybody."

"Even the saints?"

"Even the saints." Grandfather chuckled. "If you look at the word 'saint,' you'll notice that the first letter is *S*. It stands for selflessness and sacrifice. Without the *S*, you may think you're a saint, but you ain't."

"But if saints have bad thoughts, too, for gosh sakes, what makes them saints?"

94

"Because they kick the bad thoughts out. Having them in your head isn't what makes the trouble; it's letting them build a nest there. Worrying about the bad thoughts and fighting them back—that's the mistake. Kick 'em out, Son. That's the secret. If a fellow could see what goes on inside everybody else's head, he'd be perfectly happy to pick up his own marbles and go home. We're all mixtures of good and bad, saints and sinners, sometimes all in one day, and on different subjects. The secret is to keep trying to get better, not worse."

"Aren't there any nice people?"

"They're all nice, even when they're in trouble. As long as they keep trying to dig down in their basket and weed out their own bad apples."

"Sam Raffodil, Jr.," I said, "needs a whole new basket."

"Sam has some good points if you just keep looking."

"I've been looking for years. Sam's sepulcher isn't even whited."

"You're not really mad at Sam, son. You're mad at yourself."

"It sure feels like I'm mad at Sam."

But I understood a little of what my grandfather meant, all right. I was mad at Sam Raffodil because Sam was rich and had almost everything in the world that I didn't. And Sam didn't do a darn thing to deserve it. He was just born into it.

Sam Raffodil didn't have my grandfather, though. And every kid in Green Valley wished that they did. I told Grandfather proudly, "You know something, Grandfather?"

"No. What?"

"I got a lot more out of that sermon about the whited sepulcher down here at the barn with you than I ever did in church."

"Come any Sunday," Grandfather said. "No dues, no pews, no sermons, no collections. You can work it out."

Grandfather handed me the long-handled, barn-cleaning shovel and pointed to Prince's stall.

"There's plenty of singing, too," he told me.

Grandfather went off into a rollicking chorus, and I joined him as we worked together:

There'll be pie in the sky when we die,
When we die there'll be pie in the sky,
So live every day 'till you die,
And you'll still have your pie in the sky.

As Sundays go, it had been pretty decent.